MW01125532

Dying To Meet You

S.C. Stokes

CONTENTS

A NOTE FROM THE AUTHOR

Welcome to Dying to Meet You, the first title in my new Conjuring a Coroner series.

Urban Fantasy has always held a special place in my heart. The blend of magic and the modern world, along with a generous rewriting of history to add a hint of the arcane, is one of my favorite things to read and write.

Are ready to get lost in an exciting new world?

Dying to Meet You is set in New York in the year 2017. The key difference between this world and the one we live in, is the presence of magic. Where and how these worlds intersect...well, you'll have to turn the page to find out.

Enter the world of magic with Kasey Chase—she'll suck you into a realm of magic, murder, and mayhem that you won't want to leave.

I must warn you though. Kasey is far from perfect. She's an unschooled witch with unpredictable magic, a sharp tongue and a troubled past. She possesses a fierce sense of justice, and an insatiable curiosity that often gets her into trouble.

If Kasey were here, she would tell you that asking for forgiveness is far easier than asking for permission, so...buckle up; it's going to be a wild ride!

As you join Kasey on her adventure, I hope you too can look beyond her shortcomings and see her as I see her, a diamond in the rough.

Sincerely,
S.C. Stokes

P.S. Want some exclusive Kasey goodies? Sign up to my newsletter at the link below.

You will get access to all the good stuff, including exclusive short stories and cool Kasey swag. You'll also be the first to hear about anything exciting that is going on.

Join my newsletter here - https://readerlinks.com/l/959936

CHAPTER 1

In a city that never sleeps, death is a full-time job. Kasey tried not to complain, after all it paid the bills and kept the coffee flowing.

She gingerly balanced the cup carrier in one hand as she pulled open the Coffee Shack's door. As she stepped out onto the New York street, her ears were assailed with the symphony of chaos that was New York City traffic at a standstill. Horns blared as frustrated commuters came to a complete stop. A glance at her watch reminded her that she too was running late for work.

She struggled to pull her earphones from her pocket with one hand.

An explosion erupted around her.

Kasey froze, her mind slowing to a halt as oily smoke filled the sky. Her heart pounded in her chest as the realization set in. That was a bomb.

Another blast rang out. This time it was closer than the first. Kasey's headphones slipped through her fingers. Her left hand shook as she tightened her grasp on the cup carrier. People milled around, darting into nearby stores or pounding on the windows of drivers still stuck in traffic. The cacophonous blasts continued shaking the cityscape, residents flooded onto the streets as their homes and offices shuddered.

Kasey's mind was drawn to Manhattan, only a few miles away.

Kasey stopped, mid stride, her heart pounding in her chest. Sarah!

Her older sister lived downtown with her family. Kasey could only imagine how Simeon and Matt would be coping with the chaos. Simeon was only three, and Matt had just celebrated his first birthday.

Kasey rummaged through her purse. Another blast reverberated down the street. In her purse, her hand struck something hard. Pulling out her phone, her fingers trembled as she called her sister. No signal.

The ground rumbled beneath her feet, as the largest explosion she had witnessed yet reverberated through the street. Manholes burst; plumes of smoke streamed out of the portals into the air. The pillars of smoke glowed an otherworldly green as they rose skyward.

Pedestrians screamed as chaos reigned on the street. Drivers abandoned their grid-locked vehicles and attempted to flee on foot. A few of the lucky ones made it to the sidewalk. Others were overcome by the smoke surging up from beneath the road.

A thunderous peal split the air. Kasey spun to see the building she had only just left begin to split. Large cracks opened in the masonry as the tortured structure collapsed under the stress. Brick and steel rained down around her. Those on the street beside her ran for their lives.

Kasey simply stood and watched as the devastation unfurled. After all, she had seen it before, many times. This particular vision had plagued her since she was a child. The first time she had experienced it, she had been asleep at the Academy of Magic. She had woken up screaming, her body drenched in cold sweat. Later that month when the vision had repeated itself, Kasey had approached her instructors.

While clairvoyance was not unheard of in the magical community, it was a rare gift. The instructors had been puzzled. In modern history, there had never been an event of the magnitude Kasey witnessed in her vision. The destruction had laid waste to a city. If it's not an event from the past, then it must be one from the future. Its frequent repetition only reinforced her fear that it would come to fruition.

She shook her head, and the vision parted like fog lifting. The street came back into focus, and she found herself standing back outside the Coffee Shack. Car horns blared, dragging her attention back to the present.

"I said, are you alright?" a man beside her asked.

Kasey startled.

"Oh, yeah, I'm fine," she said, turning.

The man wore jeans and an orange vest and held a hardhat in one hand.

"Then would you mind moving, so I can get my cup of morning Joe?" he said, gesturing for her to move from where she stood in front of the Coffee Shack.

"I'm sorry," she answered as she ducked out of the way.

"Thanks," the man replied. "You dropped these, by the way." He held out her headphones, studying her. "Are you sure you're okay?"

"Yep. Fine." She snatched the headphones and forced a smile. "Thanks."

Her phone began ringing. She pulled it out, thankful to end the awkward exchange, and glanced at the screen. Work was calling.

Juggling the cup carrier and her headphones, she put the cell to her ear.

"Hey," she began.

"It's Bishop here."

"Hi, detective. What can I do for you this morning?"

"You on the way to the station?"

"Sure am. Just had to grab my morning pick-me-up."

"Don't bother heading in. We have a body and it's in your neck of the woods. I'd rather you came straight over."

"Can do. Where are you?" she asked, as she headed for the subway station.

"Corner of Palmetto and Fairview. We're out back."

"Palmetto and Fairview, not a problem. I'll see you in ten."

"That close huh? You wouldn't happen to be at the Coffee Shack, now would you?" Bishop asked.

"Got it in one. Glad to see that detective's badge isn't purely decorative," she said with a chuckle.

"Good to see you have decent taste in coffee. I don't suppose you could grab me a double shot survivor while you're in the neighborhood. Beats that swill they serve at the station."

"Already got you one."

"Well played, Chase. Keep this up and we might have to keep you...even after Evans comes back," Bishop replied.

"Careful, Bishop, he's your second partner this year. People are starting to talk."

"Like who? I've not heard a thing."

"Of course not," she replied. "Far too many stairs at the station. After what happened to Evans, they just aren't game enough to risk it."

Bishop sighed audibly. "I suppose I walked right into that one."

"Or tumbled down it, I guess. It depends on your point of view." Kasey laughed.

"Watch yourself, Chase. Or you'll be spending some quality time with Evans down at General."

"See you soon, Bishop," Kasey said, cutting the call.

She waved down a cab. The turn signal on the canary yellow cab flickered as it pulled over.

"Corner of Palmetto and Fairview, thanks," Kasey said as she popped the door and slid into the back seat.

Closing the door, she reflected on the circumstances that had led to her current assignment. Fleeing from her peers at the Academy of Magic, she had pursued a normal education. That road led to NYU and a degree in forensic pathology. Her hard work paid off when she earned a position working for the Office of the Chief Medical Examiner in New York.

The OCME in New York was one of the busiest on the East Coast, a fact Kasey had been well-aware of when she had applied. What she had not planned on was the closing of the Medical Examiner's offices in Staten Island and the Bronx, resulting in longer hours and an increasingly stressful workplace. She had doubled down, throwing herself at her work, and burning off her stress training for her second love, Mixed Martial Arts.

Unfortunately, she had still snapped.

Even worse, she had been at work when it happened.

She had been rummaging around in the fridge as she searched for her yogurt.

"Looking good, Chase. When are you going to let me buy you a drink?" The voice belonged to John Ainsley, a fellow forensic pathologist and resident pain in the ass at the OCME.

"Three weeks from never, Ainsley," she answered as she continued rummaging about in the fridge. "Same answer as last time you asked, which was this morning. Now get out of here. I'm not in the mood for your crap today."

Kasey had expected a witty response. John Ainsley was used to getting his way. Family money had seen to that.

Instead, his footsteps crossed the small kitchen. Kasey tried to extricate herself from the fridge but couldn't free herself before John spanked her. Her head hit the shelf.

For the first time in years, she saw red.

Her blood boiled as she flew out of the fridge, condiments and containers spilling everywhere.

"What the hell?" she started as she spun around, only to come face-to face with Ainsley as he downed a spoonful of yogurt from the container in his hand.

Her yogurt.

Before the entitled brat could respond, she drove her fist into his ribs.

The yogurt hit the floor as John doubled over, winded. Grabbing a fistful of his hair, she slammed the fridge door into his head. The door's contents scattered. John tore free of her hold, but she took two swift steps and kicked him in the chest.

The blow knocked John off his feet and into the flimsy lunch table which buckled under the weight. Kasey picked up what was left of her yogurt and crossed the room.

Without mercy, she slowly emptied the contents onto John's now cowering form. "Don't ever touch me, or my yogurt, again. Do you understand?"

John whimpered. Kasey took that as a sign of his understanding.

Unfortunately, John's family had felt differently. Kasey's beating had left John with three broken ribs and a chipped tooth. The Ainsleys had tried to press charges but Dr. Sampson, Kasey's boss and the city's Chief Medical Examiner, had countered with dismissing John for sexual harassment.

The two parties reached an armistice. In exchange for dropping the charges, Kasey would be seconded to the NYPD to consult until things died down in the office.

Kasey had been furious, at least until she discovered how much she preferred working in the field. Fieldwork with Bishop certainly beat the over-scheduling in the M.E's office.

Looking over the driver's shoulder, Kasey could see the police cordon ahead.

"Here is fine, thanks."

The driver pulled over. Kasey paywaved the fare and stepped out of the cab. Squad cars lined the edge of the corner of Palmetto and Fairview. A few officers were speaking to locals gathered on the street; others canvassed the nearby stores and buildings, likely searching for witnesses.

Active crime scenes still made Kasey a little nervous. She took a deep breath. When that failed to stop her quickening pulse, she sipped on her coffee.

"Blech. Lukewarm coffee, it's just not the same," she said to no one in particular. Sneaking a glance around, she took the risk. "Berwi," she whispered as her mind crystallized on her desire.

The arcane energy flowed to her hand, warming the coffee cup. She raised the cup to her lips. "Mmm. Much better."

The world of magic, Kasey thought as she took another sip of coffee, history's greatest secret, hiding in plain sight. People were prone to believe what they wanted to believe, and people just didn't want to believe a witch or wizard lived next door. In an age of information and technology, myth and magic were conveniently explained away or attributed to scientific advancement.

Wizards had tried to bring their world of magic into the open centuries ago, magic and the mundane living side by side in harmony. The great vision was never realized. Witch hunts burned their way through Europe, and the centuries that followed were a dark time for humanity.

As the years passed, the world of magic faded from the minds of men and the magical community was only too willing to let it happen. There was safety in secrecy. For those outside the ancient bloodlines, words are merely a method for communication. For those of magical descent, the tongues of old allowed them to manipulate and control the arcane energy coursing beneath the fabric of the world.

For Kasey, this had meant relearning the language of her ancestors. Most considered the Stonemoores to be of English stock, but Kasey knew better. Their true roots lay in hills of Caerdydd, or Cardiff as it was known today. Taught by her parents and the instructors at the Academy, Kasey had learned the difficult language and begun to access the power that came with it.

Berwi means to boil in Welsh. Had Kasey been focused on a person rather than the coffee she was carrying, its effects would have been terminal as every liquid in the target's body superheated in an instant.

The use of magic required control, which was why children from gifted families were sent to the Academy of Magic. There they could hone their gifts before they would be allowed to practice them in the wider world.

Kasey had fled the Academy and changed her name to shake her past. Elizabeth Stonemoore was the crazy girl who claimed she saw visions; Kasey Chase was a successful forensic pathologist.

A forensic pathologist flew nicely under the radar of the Arcane Council, the body that governed the actions of all magic users, registered and unregistered, in the United States of America. A simple boiling spell in the middle of New York would not be noticed. There were tens of thousands of registered magic-users in the Tri-state area. It was one of the many reasons she had chosen New York. Here, she was a small needle in a very large haystack.

"Chase!" Bishop's voice cut through the crisp morning air. "Stop dawdling and get over here."

Kasey spotted Detective Diane Bishop waving at her from in front of an alleyway that ran beside the block of apartments. In her early thirties, Diane Bishop was at the top of her game. She had spent most of her career on the streets of New York.

She was dressed head-to-foot in a black pantsuit that cut a sharp figure. Her blonde hair fell neatly to her shoulders, and her piercing brown eyes could read a perp at a glance. There was a focus and drive about her that had quickly won Kasey over.

"Is that for me?" Bishop asked, pointing at the second coffee.

"Of course, double shot survivor. Just like you like it."

Bishop accepted the offered cup and took a long sip. "Yeah, that's the one, Chase. Exactly what I needed today. Thanks."

"You're welcome. I don't want to dampen the mood, but you seemed out of sorts on the phone? What's up?"

Bishop's eyes darted back to the coffee cup. "It's the scene, Chase."

"What do you mean?" Kasey asked, a little taken aback by Bishop's skittishness.

Bishop just shook her head as she rested her cup on the hood of a squad car. She pulled her pen from inside her jacket pocket and held it up with two hands. With a flick of her wrists, the pen snapped in half, spraying plastic all over the pavement.

Kasey gulped to prevent the coffee she had just sipped from bursting out of her mouth. "What the hell, Bishop? What was that for?"

"Come with me," Bishop said, leading Kasey into the alley.

CHAPTER 2

Kasey shuffled after Bishop, a little concerned at the veteran detective's demeanor. With nerves of steel and enough grit to fill a sandbox, Diane Bishop was unflappable.

Kasey drained the last of her coffee to calm her nerves and threw the cup into one of the open dumpsters lining the alley. Spotting the aluminum case containing her kit on the trunk of the squad car, she undid the latches and flipped the lid open. Taking a moment to slide on a pair of latex gloves before picking up the case and following Bishop deeper into the alley.

"The building super found her this morning," Bishop started, pointing to a middle age man standing in front of another officer. "Came down to empty his trash and found her slumped behind the dumpster. Called it in immediately."

Several police officers sat hunched over a body that was resting against the nearest dumpster.

"Mind if we have some room, officers?" Kasey asked. "I can take it from here."

One of the officers kneeling by the body turned to her and raised his eyebrow.

"Come on, Morales, you know the drill. She's with us," Bishop said. "Give her some space."

"She's a lab tech, not a cop, Bishop. Can't you get her in a windbreaker or something? It's a little off-putting seeing a civilian poking around an active crime scene."

Kasey dismissed the comment. "I would wear one, Morales, but then we'd clash, and I think we both know I'd wear it better. I don't want your diminished self-esteem on my conscience."

She bent down to examine the victim.

"Smart ass." Morales laughed as he stood up.

"Careful, Morales, the last man to focus on that particular part of my anatomy is still nursing three broken ribs."

"The Ainsley brat?" Morales asked.

"That's the one," Kasey replied.

"So the rumors are true? Most of the precinct has wanted to do that for years. If you have enough stones to stand up to the Ainsleys and their money, you'll keep."

"Thanks for the endorsement, Morales. Now if you don't mind, make yourself scarce. You boys are blocking my light."

"Plenty of bark to go with the bite, Chase." Morales shook his head, "Alright, Johnson, let's hit the streets. See if we can't find a witness. There's more than two dozen apartments with a view to this alleyway. It's hard to believe no one saw anything."

"Thanks, Morales," Bishop said as the two officers strode toward the street. "I'm going to talk to the super, Chase. Shout if you find anything."

Kasey nodded as she set about her examination. The body was that of a young woman in her early twenties. The woman was lying against the dumpster at an impossible angle, her neck clearly broken. Her brunette hair was disheveled from her fall. An angry purple bruise had swollen the side of her face, likely caused by the impact when she had struck the dumpster. The blow itself would have hurt but it wasn't the cause of death.

Death itself had been caused by severe trauma to the neck. Kasey understood at last Bishop's pen snapping metaphor. The level of strength required to inflict such a wound was considerable, far more than movies liked to portray. It appeared the attacker had strength to spare, coming dangerously close to separating the woman's head from her shoulders.

Kasey continued her examination. The victim's fingernails were short and well-kept. In the event of a fight, a victim might have trace elements of her attacker's DNA under her nails. If there was any, it wasn't visible to the naked eye. The lab would need to do further testing.

The woman was still wearing her flannelette pajamas and slippers. Her bag of trash lay scattered in the alley. The lid of the dumpster was still raised. Whoever had attacked the young woman, had done so when she had tried to heft the trash into the dumpster.

The most likely course of events seemed that she had been jumped from behind. Her neck was snapped, and as she dropped to the ground, she had struck her face on the dumpster.

But if you were going to kill her, why not shove the body into the dumpster and hide the evidence?

The crime scene made little sense. If it was a robbery, it was a poorly planned one. The woman's attire didn't even have any pockets, so no chance of a wallet. If it was premeditated, why leave the body to be found?

Kasey had more questions than answers.

She determined to get a better look at the bruising around the victim's neck. She set down her kit and gingerly lowered the woman's body so that she was lying flat on the alley floor. As she did so, Kasey watched as a familiar haze cloud her sight. This time, it didn't catch her unaware. She closed her eyes and welcomed the vision.

When the haze cleared, Kasey hovered like a ghost in the living room of an apartment. Often in her visions, she sat as a silent observer witnessing events unfold before her. But from time to time, Kasey would experience events as if she were the victim themselves. Those particular visions hit her the hardest.

From the window, she could see the busy lights of the street below and in the distance, the brightly lit skyline of New York

City after dark. She strove to establish a timeline. Anything that might help her understand what had happened to the young woman.

Unfortunately, the scenes from the vision might have taken place days, weeks, or even months ago. Context was everything. Kasey searched the apartment but a set of keys jingled at the front door. As a key slid into the lock, movement erupted in the kitchen.

A woman appeared in the kitchen doorway. Kasey knew her at a glance: it was the woman from the alley. She was wearing the same flannelette pajamas.

It's last night. Unless she wears those same ugly pajamas every night. Darn it.

The door swung inward revealing an unkempt man in soiled overalls.

"Brad, where the hell have you been? It's almost midnight," the woman said.

"Out. What is it to you?" the man responded, his words running together.

"Oh, great, you're drunk again. It's only Tuesday. How are we even going to pay rent here if you lose your job? We can barely afford it as is." The woman grabbed a pile of bills off the table and shook them in the air.

"Money, money, money. That's all you care about. Stop treating me like I'm your meal ticket. We've been dating for over a year now."

The woman threw down the bills in protest. "I work two jobs, Brad, just to cover my share of the rent. It's hardly what I had in mind when I said I wanted to live in New York."

Brad teetered in the door before stumbling to the sofa. "Well, sorry your dream isn't what it was cracked up to be. If you put the same effort into us that you do at work maybe life wouldn't be like this at all."

"Maybe if you stopped trying to drink yourself to death, I would want to," the woman replied as she disappeared into the kitchen. She re-emerged moments later carrying a bag of trash. She crossed the narrow living room and slid into her slippers without saying another word.

"Yeah, that's right, you take out the trash," Brad said, waving his arm around. "About time you pulled your weight around here."

Turning in the doorway, the woman replied, "I'd take you out too, if I could carry you."

With that, she slammed the door on the way out. Even in her slippers, her trudging reverberated down the hall to the elevator. Kasey longed to follow her, but her vision form wouldn't budge.

It took Brad a moment for the insult to sink in.

"Trash... I'll give you trash," Brad muttered as he pulled himself to his feet.

"Kasey!" a voice called.

The mist descended, obscuring her view. Kasey blinked to clear her vision. Bishop stood over her. At her side stood the building super and two more police officers.

"What's up?" Kasey asked, tilting her head to one side.

"Mind explaining what you're up to, dreamboat? CPR isn't going to bring her back. Her neck's been snapped."

"I wasn't doing CPR, detective," Kasey replied, scrambling for an answer. "I was simply trying to get a closer look at these markings on her neck."

"And?" Bishop pressed.

"The bruising suggests she was surprised from behind."

"Anything that might give us an idea of who we are looking for?" Bishop asked.

Kasey scrambled for a means to convey what she'd learned from her vision. Clairvoyance was not a promising substitute for evidence at the NYPD. "This was an execution, not an accident, detective. We'll need to do further tests but if I were you, I'd be looking for a boyfriend or lover. Someone with an axe to grind. You get anything useful out of the super?"

"Not particularly. He mentioned a few of the tenants complaining of a domestic last night around midnight. Could be our girl." Bishop turned back to the building super. "Spencer, those complaints, which floor were they from?"

"The third floor, ma'am. Same as her," he replied, pointing to the body.

"Did anyone else share the apartment? A husband or boyfriend? Maybe a girlfriend?"

"Boyfriend. Drunken louse by the name of Brad Tescoe. They've been living here for a little over a year."

"Any idea where we can find Brad now?" Bishop asked.

"He's a mechanic somewhere in Queens. Not sure where exactly. He's normally home around five, if you want to wait for him," Spencer said.

"Oh, I don't think we'll be waiting," Bishop replied, turning to the officer beside her. "Danetto, put out an all-points bulletin on one Brad Tescoe. He's wanted for questioning. See if you can't track down his workplace. If he hasn't skipped town, he might be there."

"Sure thing, detective," the officer said before he made his way back to the squad car for a radio.

"Anything of note upstairs?" Kasey asked.

"A few of our boys have swept the apartment. Didn't find a thing. It definitely went down here in the alley," Bishop answered. "If it was the boyfriend, find me something we can use to put him away."

"Will do, detective. Give me a lab and a few hours. If he left a trace, I'll find it," Kasey said, bending back over the body for a closer look.

Kasey looked at the young woman before her. Such a waste of life. It was times like this she was proud of what she did. Sure, as a doctor she might do some good, cure a cold maybe even save a life here or there. But here on the job, every time she helped close a case, it was one more violent offender off the streets, one more opportunist behind bars. Every day she could make a difference.

She went to stand but something caught her eye. Leaning forward, she examined the bruising around the woman's throat. She reached for her kit and produced a set of forceps and an evidence bag. Leaning back over the victim, she gently lifted a hair from the woman's neck. It was short and blond, a stark contrast to the victim's chocolate brown locks.

"What have you got there, Chase?" Bishop asked.

"It's a hair. Not our victim's, either," Kasey said with a measure of satisfaction as she held the hair up for a better look.

"You think it's our suspect's?" Bishop asked.

"I doubt it," Kasey replied, her enthusiasm dying out.

"Why is that?"

"It's short and fine, so unless her dog strangled her to death, we're out of luck. It's not human," Kasey answered, bagging the hair for evidence.

"That's odd, victim didn't have a dog," Bishop answered. "No pets are allowed in the building."

"Maybe a stray wandered through this morning," Kasey answered as she stood up. "Shame the NYPD doesn't have any dog whisperers on the payroll. We could have used a witness."

"Very funny, Chase. Bag Beth for transport. We'll see what the lab shows up."

Kasey scowled. "Beth?"

"The victim. One Elizabeth Morrison. Everyone calls her Beth, or at least they did," Bishop said. "Let's get her back to the station ASAP. We need to find this missing boyfriend."

A shiver ran down her spine as Kasey looked down at the young woman at her feet. It had been almost a decade since she had changed her name, but as a child she'd always been known as Beth. Beth Stonemoore. Shaking off the unsettling tingle, Kasey dug into her kit and drew out a body bag.

Don't worry, Beth, we'll find who did this to you, Kasey thought as she unzipped the heavy-duty white plastic sheath. It had been weeks since she had seen a vision. Now she had witnessed two in a single morning. The last time that had happened had been during the carnage at the Harrington's manor.

"It's going to be a rough day," Kasey whispered to herself.

CHAPTER 3

As Bishop steered the squad car through the busy Manhattan traffic, Kasey was fixated on the victim. She couldn't help but empathize with the woman. Having seen her in vision, it was hard not to.

Kasey struggled to suppress her feelings, an unsettling combination of nerves, anger, and anticipation. Anger at how Beth's life had ended, mixed with a fear of any person capable of such a heinous and violent act. The OCME's office had felt so much more disconnected from the crimes themselves. It was different being on the front lines.

Bishop passed the time going over the facts of the case, but Kasey was too distracted.

Kasey too, had come to New York, not so much chasing a dream as she was distancing herself from her old life.

She couldn't help but think what might have happened had she been a little less lucky. She could have wound up like Beth, wrapped in plastic and riding in the back of a patrol van. She shook her head, trying to clear the macabre thought.

"What's the matter, Chase?" Bishop asked. "You don't quite seem yourself this morning."

"How do you do it, Bishop? How do you attend a scene like that and manage to go about your day like normal?"

"Experience, Kasey," Bishop replied, the corners of her mouth sagging a little. "Years of seeing the worst humanity has to offer has a way of numbing you to it. I know it wasn't a pretty sight. Are you sure that's all that is bothering you?"

"Yeah, just a bit of a slow start today is all," Kasey answered unconvincingly.

"You sure it's not the fact we just bagged a woman your age? A death like that can often cut a little close to home," Bishop said as she slowly drummed her fingers on the wheel.

"Maybe. I've had a lot on my plate lately," Kasey said, turning to Bishop. "I wasn't exactly planning on this transfer from the OCME. Don't get me wrong, I'm loving working with you, but the Ainsley stink is a little harder to get rid of than I'd first thought. Just a little worried it might plague me here too. That much money gives a person reach."

Bishop's eyes went wide as her mouth dropped open. "I thought your old boss put the clamps on that one when she shot down the assault charges."

Kasey shrugged. "She did, but you know that nagging feeling you get, when you know something isn't quite over? I feel it now. Like something is up there hovering in the sky, just waiting to fall on me like a stack of bricks."

"Well, aren't you just a little ray of sunshine," Bishop said.

"You can't talk, Bishop. I don't think I've seen you smile at all in the weeks we've been together."

The creases on Bishop's forehead only deepened. She was hiding a burden of her own. It was well concealed, buried beneath her stern demeanor, but something was there. She made a mental note to dig a little deeper next time.

Bishop turned to Kasey, as she pulled into the precinct's parking lot. "Find me something we can use to nail the boyfriend and you might just see one today."

Kasey chuckled. "You got it, boss."

She leapt out of the car and made her way over to the loading dock so that she could sign the body into the morgue. The sooner she could get answers, the better she'd feel.

The van pulled up and backed into the dock, beeping as it reversed. When it came to a stop, two officers jumped out of the van and proceeded to load the body bag onto a gurney. Kasey followed the two officers through the doors and trailed them down the hall. They rode the elevator in silence down to the morgue.

As its doors opened, she was met by the department's own medical examiner, the impossibly cheery Doctor Vida Khatri. Vida was of Indian heritage but born in the United Kingdom. The unexpected accent provided a distracting alternative from the usual East Coast accent Kasey had become so familiar with.

Vida himself was high on life, an unlikely disposition given his profession and the fact that he spent twelve hours a day surrounded by dead people.

"Oh, Kasey, you shouldn't have," Vida began, pointing at the gurney being pushed by the two officers. "And here I didn't get you anything."

"Come on, Vida. The woman just died. Show a little respect," Kasey said, following the gurney into the morgue.

"I hope so, otherwise she's gonna get a considerable shock when she wakes up in here," Vida answered with a wry grin.

Kasey knew it was impossible to try and lampoon the doctor's enthusiasm. "I guess you're right, Vida, but all the same, you might want to double check before we open her up. If the first thing she sees is you standing over her with a bone saw… well, I'm sure she'll scream loud enough to wake the others, dead or not."

Vida chuckled as he followed close behind. "Sound counsel, to be sure. I'm not quite ready to face the zombie apocalypse this morning. So, what have you brought me?"

"Deceased young woman in her early twenties, cause of death, broken neck. Obvious swelling and bruising around the esophagus lead us to believe it was not an accident. Additional bruising on the face likely occurred postmortem, probably when she hit the dumpster or pavement. The victim had been heard arguing with her boyfriend who is now missing. He is our lead suspect. We need to run a set of labs, ensure there was no other foul play. Bishop needs something we can use when they eventually drag in her sorry excuse for a boyfriend," Kasey answered matter-of-factly.

"Lovers spat, those are the worst," Vida said as the officers brought the gurney to a halt in the center of the room. "Alright, fellers, you can leave her there. We've got it from here."

The taller of the two officers, Jones, turned to the doc. "She's all yours, Vida. Find us something we can use to nail this fool, would ya?"

"That is my job, gentlemen," Vida replied as the two officers hurried out of the morgue, closing the door behind them.

Vida unzipped the white body bag and Kasey helped him lift the victim onto the steel examination table. He fussed about the body, making a cursory examination.

"I daresay you're right about the cause of death, but just to make things interesting, I'll put down a twenty and say it wasn't the boyfriend, it was someone else. A losing bet perhaps, but hey, you seem like you could use the money." Vida chuckled as he continued his inspection.

"A wound like that and you think it wasn't the boyfriend?" Kasey asked. "You're on, Vida. I'll take your money, even if it's just to teach you a lesson. You're an addict and one of these days it will be the death of you."

"Addict? Me? Never," Vida said unconvincingly. "I can stop any time I want."

"I bet you lunch tomorrow that you can't make it the rest of the day," Kasey taunted.

"Fine," Vida said. "I'll take your money. At least if I lose the twenty, I know you'll be using it to buy me lunch." He laughed as he drew a scalpel off the tray to his right.

There was a knock at the door. Kasey looked up in time to see it open partially. A blonde woman with her hair drawn up in a bun poked her head through the gap. She made as if she would enter the morgue but paused.

"Can I help you?" Kasey asked, heading toward her.

"Are you Kasey Chase?" the woman asked.

"I am. Who's asking?"

"I'm Kathleen. I'm the Chief's assistant. He'd like to speak with you, seemed rather urgent about it. Insisted I come and fetch you right away. He hoped I might find you here. I was a little confused though, we don't have your personnel records on file."

"That's because I don't actually work here," Kasey answered. "At least not yet. I'm on secondment from the OCME. The Department figured Dr Khatri could use all the help he can get."

"You tell yourself whatever you need too, Kasey," Vida called out from behind her, "but we all know you weren't exiled out here to spare me."

"Well, in any case, the chief would like to speak with you," the woman replied, pushing her glasses up her nose with one finger. "Shall we?"

"What, right now?" Kasey asked, a little concerned.

"Somebody's in trouble," Vida taunted.

"Oh, shut up, Vida," Kasey answered, throwing him a dirty look. Turning back to Kathleen, she asked, "Any idea why he wants to see me?"

Kathleen shrugged. "None at all. He took a call, and as soon as he got off, he sent me down here to find you. Your guess is as good as mine."

"Very well," Kasey answered, "Let's go see what this is about." Turning to Vida, she said, "Bishop is hustling for any evidence we can get. She needs something so we can hold the boyfriend. Feel free to start without me. Let's get Bishop what she needs." She turned back to Kathleen and gestured towards the hallway. "Shall we?"

Kathleen nodded and made her way to the elevator. She pressed the button and the doors parted. Kasey followed her inside stepped inside. When the doors closed, Kathleen pressed the button for the fourth floor and the elevator jostled into motion.

As the elevator came to a halt, she turned to Kasey. "Have you ever met the chief?"

"No, I can't say I have had the pleasure," Kasey replied.

"Well, Chief West is old school. Doesn't tolerate any foolishness," Kathleen stated.

"I'll keep that in mind. Thanks for the heads up."

The elevator dinged, and the doors swung open, revealing a small waiting area. Beyond it lay a glass wall with a boardroom and another office with its curtains drawn, preventing her from seeing within. Presumably it belonged to the chief. The desk sitting just outside the door would be Kathleen's.

Kathleen swept out of the elevator and across the small waiting room. Leaning into the open doorway, she tapped quietly on the glass before announcing, "Kasey Chase to see you, chief."

"Show her in, Kathleen," a voice called. It was firm and unyielding.

Kathleen backed out of the doorway. "Head on in, Kasey. The chief will see you now."

Kasey nodded in thanks and stepped into the office. The chief sat at his desk, pen in hand as he worked through an impressive stack of reports that were piling up. At a glance, the chief was in his early fifties, his hair, once black, was now mostly a silvered gray. His hard blue eyes bored straight through Kasey as he looked up from his paperwork.

"Miss Chase, could you close the door?" he asked

"Certainly," she said, easing the heavy glass door shut.

"Grab a seat." He motioned to the chair sitting before his heavy oak desk.

She sat down, her heart skipping a beat as she waited for him to speak.

"I'm sure you are wondering why you are here, Miss Chase," he began.

"Yes, sir."

"I'd prefer chief. I haven't been knighted...not that I know of, anyway," he continued.

"Of course, chief," she said in a hurry.

"Simply put, I just got off the phone with the Mayor."

"The mayor?" she asked, confused.

"Yes. I've been in this office twelve years and I can count on one hand the number of times the mayor has called me personally. So, when the mayor calls and asks about one of my staff who has been on the job only a matter of weeks, I take notice."

"He called about me, chief?" she asked, shrinking back into the chair.

"Indeed. Would you mind explaining why?" he pressed, his voice calm but firm.

"If I had to guess I would say it's because of my incident at the OCME."

"What incident?" he asked. "I wasn't entirely clear about the circumstances surrounding your transfer here."

"May I speak frankly?" she asked.

"The only kind of talk I have much time for," he replied.

"I was harassed, chief. John Ainsley spanked me, so I broke his ribs. If I had to guess, I'd say the Ainsleys have friends in the mayor's office. That call is their little way of telling me they haven't forgotten about me."

"Broke his ribs, you say?" the chief asked as he leaned back in his chair.

"Yes, chief. Three, I believe," Kasey responded, not the least bit repentant.

"I see. Well, the Ainsleys are going to be disappointed. I judge my staff on their merits. My opinion can't be bought with wealth and privilege. Keep your head down and your nose clean, Chase, and you'll be fine. Assault any of my officers, on the other hand, and you'll be in a cell so fast your head will spin. Do you understand me?"

"Absolutely," Kasey replied, relief flooding through her system. She didn't expect any favors but knowing the chief ran a meritocracy gave her hope. Having him as a buffer between her and the Ainsleys' wrath was better than she had expected.

The chief nodded. "Broke three ribs, huh. Not bad at all. Kickboxer?"

"Mixed Martial Arts, chief. I train every day, helps me stay focused."

"I bet it does. Well, at least we know you can take care of yourself. Welcome to the Fighting Ninth, Kasey. You're excused, but see to it that I don't receive any more calls."

"You got it, sir...I mean, chief," Kasey answered as she clambered to her feet. She pulled open the door and made her way to the elevator.

Mashing the call button, Kasey tapped her foot impatiently. The elevator couldn't come quick enough. It arrived with a ding, and its doors parted. She rode it down to the basement. When the doors opened, she came face-to-face with Bishop.

"We got him, Kasey," Bishop shouted, shaking her fist in the air.

"Got who?" she asked, still processing the bizarre meeting with Chief West.

"The boyfriend. Picked him up at work. Says he had no idea about his girlfriend."

"You believe him?" Kasey asked as she tried to read Bishop's face.

"Not at all. He's cooling in an interrogation room now. Ready to take a run at him with me?"

"I don't really know anything about interrogations," Kasey protested.

"It's a learning opportunity. You don't need to do anything. Just listen and let me know if anything he says rings false with the scene or the evidence as you saw it."

"Sounds easy enough. When are we doing it?"

"Now," Bishop replied.

CHAPTER 4

With their lead suspect in custody and not a shred of evidence, Kasey's mind raced.

Bishop stepped into the elevator and punched the button for the second floor.

"So, what have you got for me, Chase?" she began as the doors slid shut.

"Me?" Kasey's heart pounded. "Nothing yet. I'd barely walked in the door when I got dragged up to meet the chief.

"Oh, a trip to the fourth floor?" Bishop asked. "How did it go?"

"About as well as could be expected. The Ainsleys have the mayor pressuring him about me. Trying to get me fired, or run out of town, whatever they can manage."

"I bet you're glad you broke those ribs now," Bishop replied. "Makes it all a little more worthwhile."

"If I'd known this would be my reward, I'd have hit him harder," Kasey answered unapologetically.

"What did West have to say about it?"

"Not a lot, to be honest. Told me to keep my nose clean and do my job. That was about it."

Bishop fixed Kasey with a stern stare. "I've been to the fourth floor, Kasey. What else did he say?"

Kasey threw up both hands in submission. "He said if I hit one of his officers, he'll throw me in a cell."

Bishop nodded. "Heed the warning. When it comes to West, the bite is even worse than the bark. The Fighting Ninth gets its reputation from West. He sets the standard and we tow the line."

"Point taken. I'll keep that in mind next time I'm thinking of thumping someone," Kasey laughed as the elevator dinged.

Bishop led the way through the bullpen, to the interrogation rooms. Reaching the door, she turned to Kasey. "Remember, you don't need to say anything. Just sit and listen. Make sure his story checks out with our scene. If there is an inconsistency, we pick at it until his story comes apart."

"Seen but not heard. I get it," Kasey replied. Remembering Brad's drunken demeanor from the vision, she found it unlikely she'd wish to speak with him anyway.

Bishop pushed open the door. "Mr. Tescoe, I'm Detective Bishop. We appreciate you coming in."

Kasey recognized Brad immediately. He was wearing the same grease-stained overalls he'd had on the night before. Either he owned more than one pair, or he'd not changed since the day before. Judging by the odor, either option was equally likely.

"You make it sound like I had a choice." Brad ground his teeth. "You show up at my work and drag me off in the middle of my shift. What's my boss going to think?"

"Well, that depends, Mr. Tescoe. If we charge you with something, he just might think you're a murderer," Bishop replied, sitting down opposite of Brad.

Kasey followed suit and took the chair beside her.

"I ain't no murderer. I told your boys already I didn't even know she'd been killed till you all showed up. This can get a man fired, ya know."

"Mr. Tescoe... May I call you Brad?" Bishop asked.

"I'd rather you didn't." Brad shook almost imperceptibly as he answered.

Bishop didn't flinch. "Well, Brad, if your girlfriend hadn't turned up dead, none of us would be here."

"I told you, I didn't kill her," Brad spat as he leaned forward his hands slapping down on the table.

Bishop didn't flinch. "Easy, Brad. You come over that table and we'll be adding assaulting an officer to your list of charges."

"Well, stop accusing me of something I didn't do," he said, slumping back in the chair.

Bishop mirrored his tone as she replied. "Why don't you tell us what you do know, Brad? From this side of the table, it's not looking great."

"That's the frustrating part," Brad said, tears welling up in his eyes. "I came home last night. I'd been drinking. She took out the trash and I passed out on the couch. When I woke up, she was gone. I thought she'd left for work early. At least I did until you dragged me in here."

"See, Brad, that's where we have a problem. Your neighbors heard the pair of you fighting last night. Leaving that part out doesn't do much to build trust," Bishop said, shrugging.

Brad groaned as he wrung his hands. Kasey watched with interest as Bishop waited. Even without training, she knew the game. Bishop was hoping if he got worked up enough, he'd make a mistake, perhaps let something slip that would give them a lead. The sad reality was Bishop's probe was a bluff. Despite him having motive and being under the influence, there was nothing to place Brad in the alley with Beth the night before.

Brad shook his head. "Last time I checked, I'm innocent until proven guilty, so enough of this crap. You have no evidence, and you won't find any, because it wasn't me. Sure, things were rough between Beth and I, but I'd never hurt her. You have the wrong guy. So, let me go or give me my phone call, because when my lawyer arrives, your case will fall apart like the wet paper bag that it is."

Bishop's face was impassive, but Kasey knew the writing was on the wall. Brad was going to walk.

I can't let that happen to Beth. She deserves justice.

"We have a witness who saw you leave your apartment," Kasey blurted, recalling her vision. "So, we know you weren't passed out on the couch like you claim."

Brad's face fell, but only for a moment. "Well, unless your witness saw me walk downstairs and kill my girlfriend, then I'm going to say your case is just as trash as it was before."

Bishop turned to Kasey and shook her head, and then focused back on the suspect. "Alright, Brad. You're free to go. Don't leave town though."

Brad's chair ground against the floor as he slid backwards. "Oh, I'm not going anywhere. Why would I? I'm innocent." He bit his lip. "Just so you know, I passed out in the hall. I was too hammered to make it to the elevator. I might be a drunk but I'm not a murderer. Please find who killed my Beth."

He opened the door and shuffled through it.

Bishop turned to Kasey. "You didn't tell me we have a witness."

Kasey had spilled the contents of her vision without considering the consequences. "I'm sorry... we don't. I was bluffing. I just wanted to shake him."

"Bold move, Kasey, but you played our hand and now we have nothing. If we couldn't shake him today, our next attempt is going to be even less convincing. Let's hope Vida can turn up something, because right now we're done."

"Did I hear my name?" a voice called.

Kasey looked up to see Vida standing in the doorway.

"Spit it out, Vida. I'm in no mood," Bishop answered.

"In that case, would you rather the good news or the bad?" Vida replied.

Seeing Bishop's sullen face, Kasey spoke up. "Good, Vida. We'll take the good."

"Well, we're still running the labs but having just met Brad, I can tell you he's not our man..."

"How do you figure that?" Bishop replied. "Their relationship was on the rocks, he has no alibi, and the neighbors heard them arguing."

"All true, Bishop, but that man is five foot six at the most, and did you shake his hand? They're tiny. The bruising on Beth's throat came from much larger hands and a man or woman tall enough that they didn't have to reach up to do it. Remember Beth was close to six feet tall."

"You're not making any sense," Kasey replied.

Vida scurried over to the table and grabbed the case file from in front of Bishop. Pointing to the pen in her hand, he asked, "May I?"

"By all means," Bishop replied, handing it over.

Vida hurriedly sketched a crude outline of a human neck and vertebrae before continuing. "Taking into account Beth's height, if our victim were indeed strangled by someone as short as Brad. he would have had to reach up to do it. Meaning his hands would been placed like this…"

Vida carefully sketched diagonal lines from the back of the neck on an upward arc toward her chin.

"I'm assuming she was strangled from behind, which makes sense based on the scene. Certainly, if she'd have been grabbed from the front, we would have had more indication of a struggle as she fought with her assailant—skin under her fingernails and so on—but she didn't fight, because she didn't see it coming. So, Brad would have left marks much like these, but instead, the marks on Beth's neck run from a higher point at the back of her neck to a point far lower under her larynx or Adam's apple, meaning…" Vida paused for effect.

"She was strangled by someone much taller than her," Bishop concluded.

"Not necessarily," Kasey answered. "She could have been on the ground already when her neck was broken. Maybe she slipped over and hit her head and Brad simply found her and finished the job."

"An unlikely scenario given the evidence we have to deal with. Brad may be a mechanic but he's a scrawny one. The strength required to break someone's neck like that… He doesn't have it in him," Vida answered. "I doubt he's your man."

"Right..." Bishop said. "So, we have less than nothing. How is that good news?"

"Well, if he's not your man, you don't have to worry so much about that botched interrogation," Vida offered.

"What makes you think it was botched?" Kasey protested.

"The man I met in the hallway just now, he did not have the look of a man on the ropes in a murder investigation. Probably because he's innocent."

"Agree to disagree," Kasey answered, her vision still fresh in her mind. Brad had to be involved, otherwise what was her vision trying to tell her? She just needed a way to prove it.

"Still waiting on the good news, Vida," Bishop prodded.

"Well, that was it, but if you're still needing a pick-me-up, we know the perp is likely six feet tall, or more, with biceps the size of Boston. So at least it's something, and definitely more than you had this morning." Vida straightened up, looking awfully proud of himself.

"If that was the good news, what was the bad?" Bishop asked, folding her arms.

"Oh, that," Vida said, stroking his chin as if he were deep in thought. "If it wasn't Brad, Kasey owes me twenty bucks."

"What?" Bishop replied, her temper rising.

"I'll grab it later, not to worry." With that, Vida backed away until he neared the door, and then spun around and disappeared without another word.

When he was gone, Bishop turned to Kasey. "You made a bet with Vida?"

"It seemed like easy money," Kasey replied, shaking her head.

"Well, you won't do that again, will you?" Bishop replied. "Don't feel bad, most people around here have made that mistake at least once. The silly ones are the ones that keep at it."

Kasey looked away, a little embarrassed.

"You didn't..." Bishop asked.

"Yep, bet him lunch tomorrow that he couldn't go a day without gambling," Kasey answered.

"At this rate, he's going to bankrupt you."

"Maybe," Kasey replied shaking her head as she looked at Bishop, "but I'm still not entirely convinced it wasn't Brad."

Bishop's face softened as she spoke. "There's a time to follow your heart Kasey, and a time to follow your head. If there is one thing I've learned about Vida, he's not often wrong. Hidden beneath that carefree attitude, he's razor sharp. He's not perfect, but I'd not bet against him, not on a case, anyway. I think he's right on this one."

Kasey was caught between a rock and a hard place. She knew her vision meant something; it always had. She just had to work out what was missing. Kasey drummed on the tables edge. Her vision was on the tip of her tongue, but she knew better than to say a word. She had tried that before at the Academy. Even witches thought she was crazy. A normal like Bishop was likely to have her admitted to a mental facility.

"Yeah, I guess so. Back to square one," Kasey said, feigning surrender.

"Unfortunately, unless the labs show up something, square one is as far as it will go for Beth. There is over a thousand shootings in this city every year. We see a body a day, sometimes more. That's not including the accidents. Without something concrete to go on, that might be about all we can do for Beth," Bishop replied, distinctly unimpressed that such an apparently open and shut case had fallen apart before lunch.

"Well, that sucks." Kasey stood, her chair grinding across the floor. "I'm going to grab something to eat. You coming?"

Bishop glanced at her watch. "Too early for me but knock yourself out."

Kasey headed out into the bullpen. There were police and desks everywhere. As she made her way through the heart of the station, she could see Bishop's point. There wasn't a desk in the room that wasn't buried in paper and manila folders. There was clearly no shortage of work for the Ninth Precinct.

Looking at the bank of elevators, knowing what she had in mind for lunch, Kasey opted for the stairs and a minute later she was bursting through the station's large double doors and onto the city street.

There were many things Kasey loved about New York—the hustle and bustle on the streets, that there was always something happening somewhere—but what she loved most of all, was the pizza. No matter where she went in the sprawling metropolis, she could find a decent slice of pizza in less than five minutes. With time to burn, Kasey made for Stromboli's Pizza on the corner of St Marks and First Avenue.

She'd often grab a pizza and make her way down to Tompkins Square Park and laze her lunch hour away.

I better not today.

With a case to solve, she wanted to be back in the station to help Vida finish his workup. She needed a solid lead to act on.

The thought of Brad's plea as he'd left the interrogation room made her quicken her pace.

She crossed the street and made her way up to the familiar red timber and glass façade. Opting for takeout, she skipped the door and went straight for the window. She was early, beating most of the lunch rush. As good as the pizza was, dropping a large pepperoni pizza later in the day made for a poor workout, and if she were in the ring, an even less desirable experience.

Giuseppe, the store's rotund owner, was on the till. "Ah, Kasey, it's good to see you. Are you having the usual today? There is one coming out of the oven as we speak."

"Giuseppe, my friend, if I were to get anything but a pepperoni pizza here, I think it would be considered a crime."

Giuseppe chuckled as he turned to shout at his staff. "Zef, get a large pepperoni pizza for Kasey, here. The one in the second oven should be just about done."

Turning to Kasey, he continued. "Look, all the food is good here, but the pepperoni pizza"—Giuseppe held his fingers to his lips as if savoring a slice— "that is my masterpiece. There is always one cooking. If no one takes it, I eat it myself."

Kasey laughed. "Well, Giuseppe, I'll take this one for the team."

She pulled out a twenty and handed it to him.

Moments later, Zef made his way over from the ovens, pizza box in hand.

"One pepperoni pizza for you, Kasey, enjoy!" Giuseppe called as he handed over the pizza.

Kasey thanked him and began the walk back to the station. As soon as she had crossed the street, she popped the lid and drew out a slice. She licked her lips before taking a bite of the cheese-covered dough.

"Mmm. Best thing to happen to me all day," she said to no one in particular as she turned for the station.

It was only minutes before she was pushing open the precinct's large steel doors. Instinctively, she headed for the lunchroom. She knew better than to eat in the morgue. Strong stomach or not, it was better not to tempt fate.

She dropped the now half-empty pizza box on the counter. Working her way through the remaining slices, Kasey thought about her day. The vision of the attack outside the Coffee Shack, finding Beth's body, and seeing the vision of Brad from the night before. Two visions in one day. That alone had been draining. Being chewed out by the chief had just been the icing on the cake.

John Ainsley. That cretin is the bane of my existence. If I see him again, I'll break more than his ribs.

Picking up the last slice, she tossed the box and headed downstairs to the morgue.

Vida was fussing about the examination table. Beth lay where Kasey had left her.

Looking up from the table, Vida spotted the pizza slice. "Ah, I see you've bought lunch. A little early but good to see you know when you're beat."

"No such luck, Vida. This one's mine. You haven't won yet. You still have eighteen hours left." Kasey finishing the last bite of the pizza.

"Fair's fair, I guess, but it's not nice to tease," Vida replied. "Well, you are right on time to help with the autopsy. Labs will be a few hours yet."

Kasey licked her fingers as she wandered to the sink. "Yep, we need to find something, Vida. We're fresh out of leads."

Kasey scrubbed and dried her hands before making her way back to the examination table.

Picking up the scalpel, Vida prepared to make the first incision. Drawing back, he turned to Kasey. "Are you sure you want to do this? I'll understand if you want to sit this one out."

"Sit it out... Why would I do that?" she asked.

"I just thought it might be a bit awkward, that's all."

"What do you mean, Vida?"

"Well, you take away the bruising on her face and shave a few inches off her height, she could be you... or at least your sister. It's uncanny, really," Vida replied, gesturing with the scalpel.

Kasey looked down at Beth. Beside her bruised face, Kasey caught a glimpse of her own reflection in the polished table. She could see Vida's point—they had more than their first names in common.

Why didn't I see it before?

The realization only served to make her more determined. "I'm sure, Vida. I want answers."

"Very well. As you wish," Vida replied. "It's not every day you have to perform an autopsy on your doppelganger. This is weird...even for New York."

Kasey looked down at the woman who shared not only her face but her birth name.

You don't know the half of it, Vida.

CHAPTER 5

The blow caught Kasey off-guard. She was fighting to catch a breath after the surprise hit to the chest drove the wind out of her.

She'd gotten sloppy and she knew it. Her mind was still clouded with the images of Beth and her autopsy. The fear that a woman's death would go unsolved was eating at her.

The afternoon's examinations had yielded no further insights into the case, so Kasey had made her way to the gym to blow off some much-needed steam. It was going poorly.

The next jab caught her on the chin, whipping her head to the side and causing her head to swim.

Kasey reeled from the punishment. One more of those and she'd be out cold.

Shaking her head to clear her mind, she pushed thoughts of Beth's grisly murder aside.

"One battle at a time," Kasey wheezed to herself between short ragged breaths.

Her attacker closed once more. His eyes darted over her, assessing her every move, weighing her choices, waiting for any mistake that he could exploit.

She watched as the corners of his mouth crept upward into a smug grin. He was enjoying this a little too much.

Kasey dug deep; she'd trained for this but just because she could take a beating didn't mean she wanted to.

A bead of sweat ran down her face and as it fell from her chin, she launched her own offensive. She threw a left jab toward her assailant's face. The man's hands came down hard, shutting down the punch as sweat glistened on his enormous biceps. As her feint was swept away, she threw everything she had into her right fist and drove it into his stomach.

The blow hit home and Kasey felt it ripple through abs that were more like corrugated steel than muscle. She dropped, sweeping her legs through his before he knew what hit him. His legs buckled and he crashed to the ground with a deafening thud that reverberated through the room. Before he could recover, Kasey leapt on top of him, and raised her fist, ready to end him once and for all.

He slammed his hand against the ground. "I yield, damn it, I yield."

Kasey dropped her fist and let out an exhausted sigh. She rolled off Marcus and onto her back, allowing herself to come to a rest flat against the mat.

"I swear, Kasey, you have more pent-up rage than any woman I've ever met." Marcus said fighting for his breath.

"You were the one who volunteered to get in the ring," Kasey replied letting her eyes wander about the gym.

Calling it a gym was perhaps a little generous. It was an old mechanics workshop that had gone out of business. Its new owner, James, was in his late fifties. A boxer in his youth, he was determined to make a safe haven for fighters to train.

The mats were secondhand and a little faded, but they still did the job. Staring up at the ceiling Kasey could see it badly needed a coat of paint. Despite the roughshod furnishings, it was a popular haunt for boxers and MMA fighters to train for their next bout. Kasey had found it months ago. With little in the way of weights or exercise machines, it was free of most of the usual gym junkies who liked to hover around giving unsolicited advice.

No, here she could relax and work out the stresses of her day in relative peace. James' gym was only a few minutes' walk if she cut through the alleyway behind the building. It was perfect for evening workouts. She could go her hardest, throwing everything into her training, knowing she only had to make the five minute trip home before she could crawl into the shower and then collapse for the night.

Beside her, Marcus rose to his feet. "Yeah. I could see you needed it. But I wasn't gonna make it easy. One more, and I might have had you."

Kasey dragged herself off the mat and to her feet. "You keep telling yourself that, Marcus. One day it just might happen."

Marcus nudged her playfully in the shoulder. "Is that right? How about we go one more and see if it's today?"

Kasey shook her head. It'd been a long and disappointing day at the precinct. Now that she'd managed to work out some of the anxiety, she was ready for a quiet night in.

"Rain check?" she asked, undoing her gloves.

"I'll hold you to that," Marcus replied with a grin.

"See that you do" Kasey said as she ambled over to her locker. She stashed the gloves in the locker, unwrapped her hands and threw her wraps into her gym bag. Slinging the bag over her shoulder, she made her way to the door. "Later, Marcus, thanks for the round."

"Later, Kasey," he called, making his way over to the boxing bag.

As Kasey slipped out into the night, a cool breeze swept past her. It was getting late; it would be close to midnight before she reached home. Glancing down the street, she reconsidered the extra time it would take turned, and cut through the alley beside the gym.

Making her way down the alley, Kasey thought of Marcus. He was in killer shape, loved to spar, and could carry a conversation.

"Tall, dark, and handsome. He is a dangerous one. I'm going to have to watch out for him," she said to herself with a laugh.

She let the thought linger. There would certainly be worse things in the world than spending time with the charming

Marcus, but she was hardly in the mood for a relationship right now. Life was crazy enough as it was without adding the drama a guy would inevitably bring to it.

A muffled footstep caught her attention. She turned, squinting to see back down the alley. The towering residential buildings on either side cast long shadows over the narrow passage.

She searched the alley but found nothing. Convinced that her ears were playing tricks on her, she continued down the laneway. She had no doubt her trepidation was magnified by Beth's case. The poor woman had been found in an alley. A chill ran down Kasey's spine as the hairs on her neck prickled.

"Easy," she told herself. "Don't be crazy. You're almost home."

Another footstep sounded down the alley. This time it was closer. Kasey paused.

The footsteps didn't.

There was another and another. Kasey spun as a shape launched out of the shadows, bowling her over.

Kasey's gym bag hit the pavement as she tumbled to the ground beside it. Her attacker grappled with her, and she rolled, throwing him free.

She came to a stop on her back. Her assailant loomed over her. He looked to be in his early thirties and towered over her at almost seven feet tall. How had he managed to conceal himself for so long?

The man's eyes narrowed on her. They were cold and distant as he stared down his long nose at her. The man was lithe and wiry, but he moved with the speed and strength at odds with his slender frame.

Reaching behind his back, he drew a switchblade. With a flick of his finger, the slender blade emerged.

Kasey scrambled to her feet as the man closed in. The slender blade slicing through the air as he drove it toward her.

She sidestepped the thrust only to have the blade slice through her shirt as if it were paper, passing so close to her flesh she could feel its bite.

Launching her own offensive, Kasey punched the man in the stomach.

He grunted but didn't slow. Rather he brought the knife back around for a stroke designed to slit Kasey's throat. Ducking under the blow, she hit him again and again.

Quick as a whip, her attacker lashed out with a backhanded blow.

The blow struck her with enough force to spin her around. It was the same cheek Marcus had punished earlier.

As her head reeled, Kasey lamented her earlier exertions. Her attacker was fresh. She, on the other hand, was fighting for every breath.

"Why are you doing this?" she asked, struggling to find her footing.

The man said nothing. He simply raised the knife and closed once more.

As the blade plunged toward her, she grabbed the man's fist with both hands. She yanked and twisted in an attempt to wrest the blade from his grasp. With iron will, the man held fast to the knife. Slowly his other arm tightened around her, she was trapped.

Opening her mouth, she sank her teeth into the attacker's fist.

Her attacker yelped as the knife slid from his grip. It struck the sidewalk, and Kasey kicked it down the alley, letting out a satisfied grunt as the blade skittered across the concrete.

Her jubilation was short lived as her lithe assailant wrapped one arm around her throat and began to squeeze.

Kasey gasped as her air supply was cut off.

Her pulse pounded in her ears, and the man tightened his grasp. Kasey felt like her head might explode. The man possessed a strength she would not have expected. As she struggled against him, she knew she was losing the fight of her life.

In that moment, the sight of Beth's body barged its way into her mind. Was this how Beth had died? Had this same man attacked her? Or was this an unlikely coincidence?

Unable to shout for help, or even breathe, Kasey threw her elbow back into him. The blow struck home, but the man's grasp didn't budge.

She had but one course left to her. Using magic in front of a normal was against the laws of the Arcane Council but using it on a normal was even more abhorrent. The council's laws were crystal clear on this particular point but as the thug's arm steadily crushed her windpipe, Kasey didn't give a damn what the council thought.

Raising her foot, she stomped as hard as she could. She knew better than to aim for the flesh of the foot; it could take the punishment.

Instead, she Kasey aimed for the toes. The slender, tender, and easily broken toes.

The thug cried out in pain as three of his toes broke beneath her boot.

His grip slipped. Yanking down on his arm with both of hers, Kasey sucked in a quick breath.

As she exhaled, Kasey muttered the first phrase that came to mind. "Dwrnyrawyr!"

The phrase meant fist of air in Welsh but for her attacker it meant a world of hurt.

The blast launched them both backward into the alley wall. His skull cracked against the wall, before slamming into the back of Kasey's head. The sound of his nose breaking brought a smile to her pained face.

As her attacker collapsed, Kasey managed to stay on her feet, his body having cushioned the worst of the blow.

Turning, she looked down to see the thug lying in a heap, blood streaming from his broken nose.

Kasey's heart raced. The repercussions of what she had done were beginning to settle in.

She'd used magic on a normal.

For a second, she contemplated finishing the job but discarded the notion. Killing him in self defense would have been one thing. Premeditated murder was wholly another.

He deserved to rot in a cell for the rest of his life, and besides, who would believe him anyway? He would be just a thug telling stories about the girl who beat him up. Magic? No one would believe it.

The man trembled as Kasey stooped down. "Don't die on me now. I have a partner that would love to speak to you."

She backed away, as the man spat out a mouthful of blood.

His mouth twisted up into a sinister grin. "I don't think so."

Before Kasey could lay a hand on him the man whispered, "Mur d'ombres."

Oily black smoke rose from the ground, pooling about him, ebbing and flowing as it covered his wounded form. Then as suddenly as it had appeared, the mist vanished and so did her attacker.

Her jaw dropped. The man had simply vanished into thin air, leaving only a lingering scent where his injured form had just been.

She knew the scent well. After all, she was a witch.

"Magic," she muttered as she collapsed, utterly spent.

CHAPTER 6

Kasey's alarm blared loudly, dragging her from her slumber. She fumbled about blindly, seeking to put a stop to the never-ending beeping, and rolled off the couch, landing face first onto her phone. With the source of the disturbance located, she shut off the alarm. Glancing at the screen, she sighed, she was certainly going to be late to work.

The beeping had been her emergency alarm. In her exhausted state, she had slept through her usual 7 o'clock setting. She picked herself up off the floor and ran to the bathroom. Her mirror revealed the results of her evening's brush with death. An impressive bruise was forming nicely on the left side of her jaw.

Well, that didn't disappoint. Oh well, no time to worry about it now.

She hurriedly showered and dressed for work. Skipping her morning coffee ritual, she was on the subway and heading into Manhattan only twenty minutes later. Despite her rush, it was still well after nine when she pulled open the large double doors and made her way into the station.

Avoiding the elevators, Kasey took the stairs, hoping her late entrance and bruised face would go unnoticed. She made her way down to the morgue and entered the room. Vida stood next to two large men in suits. Kasey stopped, ready to back out of the door, but it was too late. She'd already been seen.

The men turned toward her.

Vida smiled.

"Ah, Kasey, good morning! Nice of you to finally join us. These two men have been waiting to have a chat with you. Now that you're here, I'll leave you in their very capable hands." Vida excused himself and squeezed past Kasey. Pausing for a moment at the door, he affected his most robotic accent and said, "I'll be back!" before scurrying down the corridor, leaving Kasey alone with the two strange men.

"Kasey, would you mind shutting the door? We would prefer our conversation remain private. You'll understand why in just a moment," the closer of the two men asked as he pointed to it.

Kasey's pulse quickened but she did her best to hide her nerves. Nodding, she slid it shut.

"Why don't you pull up a chair? We could be here for a little while," the man asked as he and his companion made themselves comfortable.

Kasey grabbed a chair from her workstation and set her purse down on the table. The man on the left was short and squat, but well-built. Kasey imagined he would pack quite a punch were he a boxer. The one on the right was lean and roughly Kasey's height.

"Mind telling me who you are and what you're doing here?" Kasey asked skeptically. "It's not every day I get visitors. I can only surmise that you are from the Mayor's office or somewhere else of that ilk. You'll be the latest attempt to make my life a misery. Behind the suits and smiles is Ainsley money. How did I do? Am I close?"

"Poorly," the taller man replied. "But not to worry, no one is keeping score here. I am Johnson, and this is Clarke. Your colleague believes us to be with internal affairs. That is, of course, a lie, but a necessary one given he is a normal."

A normal. To use that word could only mean...

Johnson finished her thought. "We're with the Arcane Council. More particularly, we work in the ADI."

"ADI? Arcane Council? Sorry, fellas, I think you might be barking up the wrong tree or barking mad. I have no idea what you're talking about," Kasey said, feigning ignorance.

Clarke replied, "Oh, I don't think that's quite true. You see, Kasey, we've had our eye on you for some time. One of our agents spotted you performing an incantation in the street and we have kept a watch on you ever since. You are, after all, not listed on the records of Council, and as such are an unregistered witch practicing magic in the city of New York.

"While registration isn't mandatory, you are still subject to the Council's laws and governance. The Council acts to protect all magical beings in the United States of America. For the most part, you've kept your head down, but your actions last night were a clear breach of council laws governing the use of magic. As part of the ADI, our job is to prevent exactly those kinds of incidents from occurring and here you are, causing them with reckless abandon."

Even though they knew she was gifted, she didn't want to incriminate herself. "The ADI, still no idea what that one means. Mind spelling it out for me?"

"Sure," Johnson replied. "It's the Anti Discovery Initiative. It is our job to ensure normals don't get any whiff of true magic being performed. It is in our best interest that our community remain hidden from the world at large. Suspicion and superstition have always been enemies of magic and we can ill afford the attention and persecution that discovery would bring upon us all. It is in that capacity that we've come to speak to you today."

"That's all well and good, boys, but I'm yet to see any ID. Arcane Council, ADI, or conspiracy theorists anonymous. Whatever the case might be, keen to see some credentials. Show me what you've got," Kasey said.

Johnson sighed and reached into his pocket. Clarke followed suit. The pair produced black flip back wallets from their suit coats and placed them on the table. Kasey picked up the first and flicked it open.

She raised an eyebrow. "Internal affairs? I thought we'd already agreed that was a lie."

"Oh, sorry about that," Johnson replied. Sweeping his hand across the table, he muttered, "Datguddiwch."

Before Kasey's eyes, the details on the ID she was holding began to rearrange themselves. In a matter of moments, it went from an ID bearing the NYPD's logo and badge number, to a security card bearing the spinning spheres that served as the crest of the Arcane Council. The photo ID was unmistakably Johnson. The card listed his credentials as an officer in the ADI."

What did they know?

Her palms began to sweat, but she tried to play calm. "ADI, ha, so it is a real thing... And you two are wizards. Well, at least we know you aren't crazy. But that doesn't account for why you're here speaking with me."

Johnson's response was immediate. "Well, Kasey, your complete lack of surprise in seeing magic performed proves to us that you are who we think you are."

"And who is that exactly?" Kasey replied

"A witch, of course." Clarke replied.

"Well, you're right on that count, Clarke. I do know magic, but as we've already covered, I'm not registered with the Council, and I have no interest in the ADI. Personally, I try to keep as much distance between me and your crazy world as possible," she said, folding her arms tightly across her chest.

"It's interesting... You say that and yet you continue to use your gifts with carefree abandon," Johnson retorted

Kasey shook her head as she placed a hand on her chest "If magic makes my life easier, why wouldn't I use it from time to time? I'm careful to make sure no one else sees or hears me casting a spell..." She paused before continuing. "I may not be a fan of the Council, but I have no desire to see the other witches and wizards I care about suffer. My family is part of your community, after all. I know all about the price of discovery and I don't need a lecture. I certainly don't need it here at my job."

"Interesting. We didn't know about your family. We always figured you emigrated from overseas, faked your identity using magic, and were hiding out here in New York," Clarke replied.

Kasey recoiled, seeking to place as much distance between herself and Clarke as she could while remaining on her stool. "Well, Clarke, you're beginning to sound a little creepy, almost stalker-ish. You still haven't told me why you are here, and I do have work to do today... so if you don't mind, get on with it, please," she added as an afterthought.

Johnson sighed. "If you insist. Miss Chase. On behalf of the Arcane Council, and under the authority of the ADI, we are issuing you with a formal warning for your conduct last night. Further violations of the Arcane Council's laws and guidelines for the practicing of magic will result in disciplinary action being taken against you. This might include but is not limited to: Deportation, incarceration, or in extreme cases, death." Johnson paused to let his words sink in. "Punishment will be determined by a jury of your peers, those whom you have put at risk through your reckless use of magic in public. Do you understand?"

The warning struck her to her core. Her hands balled reflexively into fists.

"What the heck are you talking about?" she demanded. "You haven't even told me what I did."

"Oh, I had thought we were all on the same page with that one," Clarke replied matter-of-factly. "Last night, you let off enough magic in that alleyway to wake half of Brooklyn. Are you going to deny that you were there? We are here talking to you because there were half a dozen witnesses in the adjacent buildings that described you precisely. By their accounts you almost blew a man through a wall."

Kasey fidgeted nervously. It was moments like these that she regretted dropping out of the Academy of Magic. With little real understanding of how its regulatory body, the Arcane Council, functioned, she had largely avoided interacting with them. Clearly avoidance wouldn't continue to work for her now.

"I see that you have the good sense not to deny it," Clarke replied. "That saves us a lot of time."

"I was fighting for my life," Kasey answered.

"Oh really?" Clarke responded, leaning in. "Do tell."

"I was walking home when a man attacked me with a knife. He would have killed me if I hadn't hit him with that spell."

"Using magic against a normal, in front of buildings full of witnesses," Johnson asserted. "Your magic is not a toy to be paraded before the masses."

"Don't give me that. He was a wizard, and a killer," Kasey blurted, shaking her finger at the wall of steel morgue drawers. "His last victim is over there in that drawer. If I hadn't used my magic, you would be talking to a corpse right now."

Johnson interceded. "That might be true, but it still doesn't negate the fact that we were forced to spend most of last night wiping the memories of those who witnessed your little display in the alley."

"It wasn't all me. He was using some kind of spell to melt into the shadows." Kasey answered, her lip quivering. "What happens now?"

The men exchanged looks, and then Clarke said, "See that you don't cause any further issues for the Arcane Council, Miss Chase. The ADI tends toward leniency for first offenders, but repeated violations of the Council's edicts will result in punitive action. Are we understood?"

It was better than Kasey had hoped for. She had expected immediate reprisal for being an unregistered witch. To escape with only a warning, that she could live with.

"I get it. I will be more careful next time," she said.

The two agents stood up, picked up their IDs from the table, straightened their suits, and walked to the door.

"There isn't to be a next time, Miss Chase," Johnson answered, opening the door.

As the men departed, Kasey breathed an audible sigh of relief.

That could have been worse.

"I need a cup of coffee," Kasey said to the still empty morgue. As she stood to fetch a cup of the ground dirt that passed as station coffee, a familiar voice bellowed down the hallway.

"Kasey, where are you? I've been calling you for hours. We have another body..."

CHAPTER 7

B ishop stormed into the morgue. "There you are. Why haven't you been answering your phone?"

Kasey pulled out her phone and saw a half dozen missed calls. In her haste to get out of the house, she hadn't even checked her messages. Clearly, it had been another early start for Bishop.

"I'm sorry. I was just dealing with the boys from the Ar...Internal Affairs," Kasey said.

"Internal Affairs?" Bishop asked, her eyes narrowing. "What did they want with you? You're not even a cop, and what on earth happened to your face?"

"I was training in the gym," Kasey lied, not wanting to mention her brush with the murderous wizard, "Internal Affairs grilled me about my role here in the Department, working cases with you, and policy and procedure for handling evidence. Apparently, they had received a tip about possible misconduct and were just following it up. If I had to guess, I would imagine the Ainsleys were behind it."

"That family has some serious pull," Bishop said. "First the mayor's office, and now Internal Affairs. I'm guessing tomorrow it will be The White House."

"I hope not," Kasey said. "If John Ainsley has that kind of reach, I'll be fired for sure."

"You can't let it get to you, Kasey. We have more important things to do," Bishop replied, her hand resting on her hip.

"Speaking of which, you mentioned another body?" Kasey asked, abandoning her coffee plans.

"Yeah, I was on scene this morning," Bishop replied as she made her way over to Kasey. "Might be something but it could be nothing. The boys are bringing the body in now."

"What do you mean 'could be nothing'? Obviously, you suspect something. Come on, out with it," Kasey prodded

"The victim, one Brandy Cahill, was killed in the early hours of this morning in a hit-and-run. It's possible that it was just an accident but based on where we found the body and a lack of damage to the adjacent building, the driver certainly knew they had hit something. It's also unlikely she died instantly, and yet we received no emergency calls to attend to an accident in the area. It's almost as if she was run down on purpose and the perpetrator hung around to ensure no help would be forthcoming. Sounds a little crazy, I know, but I've seen stranger things in my time on the force. I'm definitely leaning away from accident and toward foul play on this one." Bishop drew a deep breath.

The elevator down the hallway dinged, likely signaling the arrival of the body. A moment later, the doors opened, and two officers emerged, pushing a gurney. The officers wheeled the body into the room.

The officers backed away. "It's all yours, detective. We are still searching the scene for evidence. We're hoping that a nearby camera might have caught something, but so far, no leads. We'll let you know if we find anything."

"Thanks, Jones, see you upstairs."

"Alright," Kasey exclaimed, striding over to the gurney. "Let's see what we've got here."

Kasey unzipped the white sheath and was confronted with the body of a young woman. "Give me a hand here, Bishop. I need to get her out, so I can see what we're working with."

Together, Kasey and Bishop lifted Brandy, and set her on the morgue's steel examination table.

A familiar mist clouded Kasey's vision.

As the mist cleared, Kasey found herself moving through suburbia. She didn't recognize any familiar landmarks. In the distance, she could vaguely make out the lights of the New York City skyline but at this size, it was clear they were some distance away.

I must be in the outer suburbs.

Looking down Kasey found she was wearing yoga pants and a light jacket. In that moment, Kasey knew she was experiencing this vision from the woman's point of view.

These are the worst.

She hated it when her gift manifested in this incredibly personal and, in Kasey's opinion, invasive extreme.

It was bizarre to be trapped in another person's body, unable to move of her own volition. Kasey forced to simply be along for the ride. The woman was listening to some jazz and blues as she jogged quietly through the streets. At least she has good taste in music. It could be far worse.

Unfortunately, the blaring music drowned out Kasey's ability to hear anything going on around Brandy. In the predawn light, it was also difficult to make out much of the environment due to the poorly lit street.

The unfamiliar environment, low light, and background noise was making it quite difficult for Kasey to gain any form of background information for the vision she was seeing. As she had become all too familiar with, context was everything to the prescient. For the most part, she might catch only the slightest glimmer of useful information. It was made meaningful by the context she witnessed in the fleeting visions.

Aside from the pervading sense of danger, Kasey was thoroughly enjoying a morning jog in which she had to put in zero of the effort required. In the distance, she spied a set of headlights. The car drew nearer, a silver sedan cruising along the quiet suburban street. With Bishop's words echoing in her head, Kasey knew what was about to happen.

She panicked.

The vehicle's headlights blinded her, rendering yet another sense worthless. Brandy closed her eyes...

Kasey fought the urge to scream, knowing it was only a vision. Such a scream would be difficult to explain to Bishop who was likely still standing beside her and confused at her lack of response. The scene before her felt so very real, and for the victim lying before her in the morgue, it had been.

Then Brandy opened her eyes and the car was gone. Just another early bird. As many times as she had witnessed these visions, Kasey still struggled to understand what she was experiencing. It was like trying to guess a random number between one and a hundred. Sometimes dumb luck would help see her get it the first time, but most of the time she found herself just blindly fumbling around, hoping for the best.

Kasey anxiously hunted for any sign of context that might aid her.

Suddenly, the world was upside down. Something had struck Brandy, hard.

Kasey was grateful she could not feel what the victims in her vision experienced.

She went dizzy as her vision spun. Houses, bushes, the road, the sky. All spun by at mind boggling speed and then it all stopped. Kasey's vision went black as the woman blinked. She was straining her eyes but all she could see was the sky above and bright lights. The woman was lying on the pavement. Two bright lights obscured most of her vision.

Kasey tried to focus but it was difficult, the glaring lights belonged to a car. The silver sedan she had seen earlier. Focusing on the number plate, Kasey seared it into her memory. EZY 8055. The music had died; presumably because Brandy's phone had been damaged in the fall. Kasey could hear the pain in Brandy's voice as she groaned in agony. Not for the first time, Kasey was glad she couldn't feel the pain of those whose visions she shared. The car door opened, and Kasey sought to get a glimpse of the driver, but it was impossible. The bright headlights made sure of that.

The woman's eyes closed once more, and Kasey's vision clouded over.

"Kasey are you still with us?" a voice called. It was Bishop.

Her vision cleared, and she found herself back in the morgue, standing over the young woman's body. Kasey was still holding her shoulders where she had lifted the young woman out of the body bag.

"Kasey?" Bishop asked.

"Yes, sorry. I was just thinking about the victim."

"Care to share with the class?" Bishop asked. "You kind of zoned out for a while there. Thought you were daydreaming on me. Kind of a weird place to be doing it, though."

"Not daydreaming, just thinking. That is my job, isn't it?" Kasey asked, putting Bishop on the defensive. Better to shift the attention back to the case.

Bishop smiled. "Indeed, it is. Fill me in. What had you so entranced?"

Kasey looked down at Brandy. "Well, the victim was hit by a car, as you mentioned. Even without a thorough examination that much is evident." Picking up a pair of scissors from a nearby tray, Kasey began to cut away Brandy's clothing to illustrate her point. Moving around the table she started at her left leg.

"This hip is likely broken. That will be from the impact of the car. The surrounding bruises are consistent with being struck at speed. The height at which she was struck is indicative of a small sedan." Kasey moved further up Brandy's body. "This bruising on her upper body, along with the cuts and abrasions on her arms and head will be from her body striking the car and then being thrown forward onto the sidewalk."

"How do you know she was on the sidewalk?" Bishop asked. "I didn't say anything about the sidewalk."

"No, you didn't," Kasey said, kicking herself for the slip up. "But the nature of the abrasions did. Had this woman struck the asphalt of the street, the cuts would have a different shape and pattern. There would also be trace amounts of it in the wounds. And while there certainly is some dirt in there, I've not seen anything that leads me to believe she ever struck the road."

Bishop nodded appreciatively at the insight. "You are right, of course. We found her on the sidewalk. The car would have had to mount the curb to hit her. Probably a drunk driver."

"How about the scene?" Kasey asked, choosing her words carefully. "Was it indicative of an accident? As you said earlier, if it were a drunk driver, there would be copious evidence. Was the car there when the body was discovered?"

"No, the car was already gone when we arrived," Bishop replied.

Kasey pressed on. "Surely a drunk driver would have careened into a tree, or a fence or something. The subsequent noise would have drawn neighbors and witnesses. Were there any of those?"

"Only the man who found her. Came out to collect his paper and found her lying there. Called us immediately but she had been dead for at least an hour, maybe more."

"Well, she may have been hit by a car," Kasey began, "but it was no accident. It was murder. The killer had likely mapped out the route beforehand. Otherwise, they simply got lucky and went unseen, but the former is far more likely than the latter."

"I gathered that much; can you give me anything that might help us identify who did this?" Bishop asked Kasey.

"Not until we've conducted a more thorough examination. That could take hours. Sorry to say, but now, good old-fashioned police work is your best bet on this one," Kasey lied. She already had the license plate of the vehicle responsible, but there was no way of giving that info to Bishop without arousing suspicion or coming across as a crazy person.

She could only hope that Bishop was able to track down the lead herself. Perhaps a traffic camera might have caught the murder, or at least the getaway.

"Alright, Kasey, well, keep me posted. I'll head up to the bullpen and run down other avenues. We still need to speak with the family. Perhaps they might know who would have wanted to do this."

"Will do, detective."

Bishop strode purposefully out of the morgue, leaving Kasey alone with her thoughts.

"What a week," Kasey said to no one in particular.

To think it was only Wednesday was a little depressing. Working at the station had a far different pace to what she had experienced at the OCME. Between visiting crime scenes and assisting Vida with the autopsies, it was proving exhausting. Added to that, the continued pressure from the Ainsleys, the attention from Chief West, and now the censure from the ADI and the Arcane Council, Kasey was feeling particularly exhausted. All her issues were compounding with a throbbing headache she was sporting from last night's encounter with the deadly wizard.

It was making for a truly awful day.

In her moment of self-pity and reflection, Kasey didn't hear the footsteps until they were right behind her.

"Well," the voice began, "if this isn't a case of déjà vu, I don't know what is."

CHAPTER 8

Kasey almost leaped out of her skin on hearing the voice. Spinning toward the door, she came face-to-face with Vida.

"Whoa, Kasey, it's just me. Told you I'd be back. What happened to the scary men in suits? And while we're at it... What happened to your cheek?" He pointed at her face.

"Sorry, Vida, I didn't hear you come in. Yeah, the suits are gone, have been for almost an hour now. Why were you so skittish around them? They were just Internal Affairs."

"Police investigating other police officers. I don't know, something about them just seems off." His gaze returned to her swollen cheek. "Speaking of things being off, I'll ask again: what happened to your face?"

"Oh, that?" she answered, gingerly touching her jaw. "Practice fight in the gym. I train most nights."

"Boxing?"

"Mixed martial arts," she answered.

"Impressive, much like that bruise. Hope you gave as good as you got," he said with a wink.

"Oh, you should see the other guy," she replied, picturing the wizard's broken nose. "I assure you he is just as sore as I am this morning."

"I'd expect nothing less," Vida replied as he circled the examination table.

"What did you mean, déjà vu?" she asked.

"Are you kidding me?" He pointed to the body on the table. "Look at her. She could be the sister of the one you brought in yesterday. A little older perhaps, and her hair is a darker, but if you look at the roots, you can see she has been dyeing it. Similar bone structure in her face. You're telling me she is no relation to Beth from yesterday?"

"Not as far as I know," Kasey said. "According to Bishop, her name is Brandy Cahill. I've not had a chance to do any digging, but on the surface, it appears not. Why?"

"They are awfully similar in appearance, both have died violently in unnatural circumstances, and both of them in a short window of time. It could just be coincidence, or we could be looking at victims of the same killer," Vida concluded.

"I doubt that," Kasey said. After almost being choked to death, Kasey was confident her wizard was the killer, and he would have been nursing his wounds, not hunting his next victim.

"How can you be so sure? Vida raised his eyebrow.

"Call it a hunch." Kasey answered.

"I hope you aren't still gunning for Brad, Kasey, I don't think he killed Beth and he certainly had no motive to kill Brandy. So, either we are looking for two unrelated killers, or if these young women keep showing up on our table, I'm going to suggest we are only looking for one," Vida said. "If you don't believe me, let's get out Beth. We haven't released the body yet. Let's put the two side-by-side and see."

"See what?" she asked.

"See if there isn't some substance to my theory," he said. "I would have thought you would have wanted to be sure. If there is a serial killer running around Manhattan, and these girls are his or her type, then you might just find yourself in the killer's crosshairs. After all, the three of you are far more similar than you are different."

A chill ran down Kasey's spine. She had dismissed Vida's serial killer theory when she had first heard it, but it certainly cast much needed light on her ambush in the alley. She had supposed it was a chance encounter but now that Vida mentioned it, she couldn't get rid of the uncomfortable sensation that something was off.

A serial killer.

It was difficult to believe that both young women had been killed by the same person, or that her attacker had recovered sufficiently from her beating to kill Brandy only hours later, though.

She made her way over to the morgue drawers. Flipping the latch, she pulled out the drawer housing Beth. Vida wheeled over a second examination table, and together Kasey and Vida lifted Beth onto it. Moments later, the two bodies were resting side-by-side and Kasey could see exactly what Vida was talking about.

Both women were close to six feet tall, with brown eyes and dark hair. The similarities ran deeper still. Both young women had high cheekbones and slender noses. There were subtle differences—the shape of their ears and complexion of their skin—but one could certainly be forgiven for thinking the two were related. As Kasey ran through the comparison and added herself to the mix, the evidence started to come together.

"I see what you mean, Vida, but how do we tell if this is merely a coincidence or a series of victims bound together?" Kasey gestured at the women lying before her.

"That part is more difficult," he said. "I usually leave it to the detectives. Normally there will be a whole string of victims before anyone manages to put two and two together. New York City is a big place. It's rare for a killer to choose multiple victims located so close together and in so short a place in time.

"Either they don't think anyone will notice or there is something driving them. and their choice of targets. In any event, it's hard to know for sure until we learn more about both of them." Vida pointed at Kasey. "In the meantime, you ought to be careful."

"Ha, ha, ha," Kasey replied, brushing Vida's finger away. "Don't worry, I haven't been out looking for love or hitchhiking recently, so I'm sure I'll be fine."

"Were they, Kasey? Don't be so dismissive. Stranger things have happened before." He settled his gaze on her. "Do you think we should tell Bishop?"

"I think we should leave the detective work to her, Vida. If there was merit to our theory, I'm sure she would have said something already. She's attended both scenes, met the victims, and has a career full of experience as a homicide detective. Moreover, I'll bet she won't want to hear such an out-there proposition without some evidence to back it up. It always comes back to the evidence with Bishop."

Vida's ears perked up and he looked at his watch. "Speaking of bets, Kasey, if I'm not mistaken, it has been twenty-four hours since you made your last one with me. True to my word, I have not made one with anyone since, so I believe that means..."

Kasey cut him off. "Yeah, yeah, I see where this is going."

"Lunch, Kasey, that's where this is going. So where are you taking me?" he asked, practically glowing at his victory.

"Fair is fair. Lunch is on me. What do you want to eat?"

"Well, you did tease me with that Stromboli's pizza yesterday. I think I could go for one of those," he replied.

"Sounds good to me, but you'll have to pick them up. I have a stack of paperwork to get through here, and I need to get started sooner rather than later." She wandered back to the counter and grabbed her purse. Rummaging through it, she found her wallet. Opening her wallet, she drew out her credit card and handed it to Vida. "Take this, though. Get anything you want and a pepperoni pizza for me."

Vida accepted the card. "You know, Kasey, one in sixteen adults in the USA had their ID stolen last year. You should really think carefully before handing over your credit card."

"You worry too much. Besides, what are you going to do? Steal my ID and use my gym membership?" She looked him up and down. "I don't think so. Besides, if you did, I wouldn't have to go very far to report you. In fact, it might just be the shortest journey from workplace to lock-up in the history of the Fighting Ninth."

Vida pointed to the bruise still prominent on Kasey's face. "Then again I wouldn't dream of it. My spirit of self-preservation is far too great."

Vida sauntered out the door, laughing.

As soon as Vida disappeared, Kasey sprang into action. She had no intention of doing her paperwork, but she did need a few minutes of unsupervised time on Vida's computer. She had intentionally used the word 'bet' in the hope he would remember their earlier gamble. Fortunately, Vida's love of pizza had led him to miss the gambit.

She walked over to the door leading to Vida's adjoining office. She tested the handle. It was unlocked, and she entered the small office. Stepping around the desk she slid into Vida's office chair and moved the mouse back and forth. The computer whirred to life, but she was confronted with a login screen bearing the NYPD's crest.

"Darn it," she exclaimed as she began rummaging around the desk for any indication of his password.

She checked the back of the monitor and scanned the desk for post-it notes. No luck there. Rummaging through the desk turned up little of use. As she scanned the office, her eyes locked on a copy of General Anatomy, the core textbook familiar to any student of Forensic Medicine. Kasey's own copy had been used to death while she was at college. Vida's, on the other hand, was in surprisingly good condition.

By now, he would have long since mastered and memorized its contents. The other books on the shelf were all post-graduate level. General Anatomy stood alone in its simple content. Kasey grabbed the manual and flipped it open. Eagerly, she scanned the front page. Nothing. She flipped to the back.

Neatly printed above the bar code in black pen was a series of twelve letters and numbers. The casual observer might have believed it a part of the bar code itself. Kasey knew better.

She punched the twelve digits into the box on the screen and pressed enter. The computer unlocked.

She scanned the desktop and found the shortcut to the program she was looking for, then double clicked it. Once it loaded, she typed in the plate she had seen in her earlier vision. E-Z-Y-8-0-5-5. The vanity plate was easily remembered. It spelled out 'easy boss.' She hit enter.

The computer hummed and Kasey held her breath. After only a few moments, a box flashed open on the screen.

EZY 8055

Registered to: Lincoln Strode

Address: 65 Hudson Road Bellerose, New York.

"Well, well, well," she muttered, rubbing her bruised cheek. "I'll be seeing you tonight, Mr. Strode."

She shut down the program and logged off the computer. Ensuring Vida's copy of General Anatomy was back where she had found it, she slipped back into the morgue just in time to see Vida making his way into the room. He was weighed down by a pair of large pizzas from Stromboli's.

He handed Kasey the top box and her credit card. "Your card, milady. The Khatri foundation appreciates your most generous donation. You are an inspiration to Medical Examiners everywhere."

Kasey shot him a look. "I live to serve, Vida. Now eat your pizza before I take it."

They discussed the case while they devoured the delicious pizzas, hypothesizing over possible links between the two women. Kasey's participation in the conversation was only half-hearted, though. Her thoughts kept reverting to her vivid vision of being run down by the silver sedan. Each time, the same mental image surged to the front of her mind.

I'm coming for you, Lincoln Strode.

CHAPTER 9

K asey wanted answers. It was almost six pm. She'd been waiting impatiently in her car for an hour. She still hadn't seen a sign of Strode.

Kasey preferred the subway, parking in New York was a nightmare. Tonight, she was in a hurry though, her car was the quickest way to Hudson Road, and she was in no mood to wait.

The streetlights around her came on, Number 65 Hudson Road remained dark. It was a quaint little two-story suburban home. White with green shutters and a chimney, it looked every part like a child's dollhouse. The image was only reinforced by the two immense homes that neighbored it. There was no car in the driveway and not a single light on inside the home. Perhaps he isn't home yet. Or maybe he just ditched the car and is laying low.

Kasey's fingers drummed ceaselessly on the steering wheel, the memory of her vision still playing in her mind.

"What makes a person do something like that?" she asked herself as she waited. What had Brandy done to earn the killer's attention.

Sitting outside of Lincoln Strode's home, Kasey wasn't sure what she had expected to find. Perhaps the silver sedan with a battered hood, or perhaps Lincoln standing in his driveway hosing away evidence as he cleaned his car. She found none of those.

Instead, the sleepy little suburb of Bellerose was quiet. Families were just sitting down to dinner. Kasey considered breaking into the home but thought better of it. After her misfortune at Brad's, she really couldn't risk any more attention at work...or from the Arcane Council. The suited grunts that served the ADI had been more than clear on that front. Further use of magic against normals would be met with harsh punishment.

Unsure of how to proceed, Kasey opted for the direct approach. She fished a NYPD windbreaker off her back seat and slipped into it. Of course, she had no ID to go with it, since she wasn't technically a part of the NYPD. Unwilling to let such a minute detail get in her way, she borrowed a trick from the ADI's repertoire.

She drew her wallet, looked at her license, and whispered the spell, albeit in her own tongue. "Cuddio."

The card morphed from her New York State issues license into an NYPD ID badge. The badge number wouldn't pass muster, but at a glance, the ID would fool most casual observers. It wasn't a true transformation, simply an illusion. One that would only last for an hour or so, at best.

It will have to do.

She slid out of the car and approached the house, making her way up the sidewalk to the front door. It was a cool September evening and she was grateful for the windbreaker. Approaching the green front door, she pulled the windbreaker tighter around her. She rapped three times on the front door and waited. There was no response.

She knocked again, louder this time. "Mr. Strode, it's the NYPD. We have a few questions we would like you to answer."

She waited. Still no answer came from within the home.

What would she do if Strode answered the door? She summoned her power in preparation. It never hurt to take precautions, and having come so far, she wasn't willing to leave empty-handed.

"If I could only get a look inside," she muttered. With two bodies in the morgue and her own attack, there was too much at stake. She needed answers and she couldn't ignore the nagging sensation in her stomach.

Something wasn't right. She crossed the lawn in front of a small garden and made her way down the driveway toward the backyard and garage.

She tried to sneak a glance in the window, but all the curtains were drawn.

With a glance around to verify no one was watching, she hopped over the fence, landing lightly in the backyard. There were still no signs of life anywhere. She approached the back entrance. Without any light, it was difficult to see inside the home. She gingerly tested the door. It was open.

What would Bishop think?

She was sure Bishop would be mortified if she'd known the truth of what had happened last night, but even more so by what she had planned right now. Bishop was by the book; she got a man with evidence and the rule of law. What Kasey was doing crossed that line, and she knew it, but she forced the thought from her mind.

I'm only trying to catch a killer.

Lincoln Strode had already killed one woman that she knew of. From looking at his entry in the licensing database, Kasey was forced to admit that perhaps Vida was right. At six-foot-six, Lincoln Strode would have been more than capable of inflicting the wounds she had witnessed at Beth's autopsy.

Brandy and Beth both bore a striking resemblance to her, and her visions only strengthened the connection Kasey felt with them. If a serial killer were at work, then Kasey certainly fit his growing profile, making her attack last night all the more dangerous. It may not have been a coincidence. The wizard might have found exactly who he was looking for.

Trusting her instincts and her extensive knowledge of self-defense, Kasey eased open the back door and entered the home.

She found herself in the kitchen. It was dark and dishes were piled in the sink. A fly buzzed around her face, and she swatted at it. A plate of leftovers sat half-eaten on the kitchen countertop. Realization dawned on her: the serial killer could be loitering inside the house.

She took a deep breath to calm her nerves but gagged as a rancid stench filled her head.

She held her breath and moved past the kitchen and into a hall leading toward the front door. On her left, a staircase ran up to a second floor. On her right, a doorway led through to a living room. Approaching the front door, Kasey poked her head around the banister and looked upstairs. The second floor was completely dark. She opted to explore the living room instead.

She rounded the corner and then stopped abruptly. There on the floor before her lay Lincoln Strode... Or what was left of him.

Kasey recognized him from his driver's license photo. Fortunately for Kasey, his face was one of the few parts of him left intact. Lincoln looked like he'd gone three rounds with a rampaging black bear. A large gash had been torn in his midsection, while a host of other cuts and bruises covered his body.

"Gee, Bishop is going to love you," Kasey muttered. "She loves a good mystery."

The thing that perplexed Kasey the most was the age of the body lying before her. Without an autopsy, it would be difficult to determine the exact time of death, but the body was exhibiting all the signs of a corpse that had been in its current state for some time, likely days. The first signs of decay were evident and accounted for the stench Kasey had been fighting since she walked in the door.

She fought the urge to throw up.

"If you are Lincoln Strode, who was driving your car this morning?" She glanced at the corpse. "You're in no condition to drive, big fella."

With a grimace, she stepped over the body and into the living room. The room itself showed no signs of a struggle. Neither was there any indication that the home had been burgled. If Lincoln had died in a home invasion gone wrong, Kasey would have expected to see the drawers and bookshelves ransacked as the burglars hunted for items of value. Instead, everything remained in its proper place, a little disheveled and untidy perhaps, but certainly not ransacked.

A pile of paperwork on the coffee table drew Kasey's attention. More than two dozen manila folders sat neatly stacked atop each other. In the slovenly hovel, the well-ordered pile of folders stood out. Kasey hurried over, picked up the first, and slid out the contents.

A picture of Beth Morrison stared back at her. The picture had a large red cross drawn over it. Also, inside the folder were dozens of documents profiling Beth and her schedule. It detailed her shifts at a local diner, the yoga class she attended each Thursday, and information about her boyfriend, Brad Tesco.

Kasey dropped the folder and grabbed the next one. Fearing what she would find, she flipped it open. As expected, it contained the image of Brandy Cahill. This image too had been crossed out. The photo featured Brandy running. In the folder were several maps of New York City. Each map had a route traced in red marker. Presumably the routes Brandy favored on her runs.

Kasey skimmed through the other notes in the file. Brandy wasn't a New York City native. According to the file, she had recently moved to New York from the West Coast to study at NYU. She was aspiring to be a lawyer, a dream that would go unrealized in the wake of the morning hit-and-run.

Kasey drew the next folder. This time, it showed a young woman at a bar pouring drinks. Unlike the first two, this one bore no red marker. She was still alive. If the killer were working in order, she would be next. Underneath the photo was scrawled the name Trudie Sears.

According to the notes, Trudie worked as a bartender at The Drift, a popular bar in Brooklyn. The bar was only an hour away and Trudie would soon be starting work.

Whoever was hunting these young women could be on their way right now. Kasey knew she needed to warn Trudie and come clean to Bishop. She needed to see these folders at once.

Each folder represented a potential target that had been surveilled by the killer. Each and every one of these women were at risk. Kasey couldn't protect them on her own. For that, she would need the NYPD's resources, and they would certainly need this information to solve the case.

She would have to manufacture a reason for being inside Lincoln's house. It would be easy enough to produce some clues that led her here, knowing what she knew now and filling in the blanks from her vision of the hit-and-run. Doubtless a missing person report had been filed for Lincoln. If there were enough dots to join, hopefully Bishop wouldn't delve too deep into Kasey's trail. Particularly when Kasey needed her focused on saving the lives of these young women.

Images of Beth and Brandy lying side by side on the morgue's cold steel table filled her mind.

I don't want to see anyone else join them.

Kasey picked up the pile of folders and started for the door. She halted, heart leaping into her throat.

Standing in the doorway was a towering beast. Kasey's eyes inched up the beast's body. She was close to six feet tall, but the beast in the doorway stood head and shoulders above her.

The beast's long hind legs joined a narrow waist. The beast's torso widened considerably, and it was immensely muscular. His golden fur did little to conceal its tremendous strength. The beast's arms, braced against each side of the doorway, were poised to tear through the fragile timbers. Atop its broad shoulders rested a wolf head.

A werewolf head.

The beast's mouth opened, and a low growl emanated from deep within. Two wicked rows of teeth lined the its jaw. As Kasey watched, a glob of saliva rolled off the end of a razor-sharp tooth and dropped to the floor.

But most harrowing of all were the eyes. They were dark red spheres that burrowed straight into Kasey's soul, savage and cunning at it watched its prey—her.

She glanced around, looking for an escape, but the beast barred the only way out. It had trapped her.

Her feet felt like concrete, while her heart raced a million miles an hour. Suddenly, the golden-brown hair she had found at the scene of Beth's murder made sense. The realization cut through her like a knife. If the beast was capable of doing that to Beth, one wrong move would see Kasey join her in the morgue.

It was moments like this that made her wish she'd carried a gun. She'd considered it when she had begun working for the NYPD, but she had always known if push came to shove, she had both her martial arts and her magic to back her up.

Unfortunately, with the visit from the Arcane Council, Kasey worried about exercising her gifts. Not while she had any other choice remaining. Werewolves were a part of the magical community, but Kasey had no idea if that would make a difference to the Council.

The beast growled and launched itself into the room.

Kasey willed her legs to move. Adrenaline kicked in as she searched for a weapon. Glancing from the charging beast to the folders in her hands, she turned and hurled the pile of manila folders at the beast. Paper and folders flew everywhere. The beast lunged. Its right claw tore through the air. She managed to duck under the blow, then punched the beast in what had to be its ribs.

The beast growled and lashed out with its other arm. The backhanded blow knocked Kasey off her feet and onto the floor. As the beast crossed the room, Kasey struggled to her feet. She ripped a picture off the wall and hurled it at the beast. The giant wolf swatted it to the floor. The picture shattered, sending glass and splinters in every direction.

Kasey grabbed a floor lamp from beside the sofa, yanking the plug from the wall. She smashed the head against the floor, busting the bulb, and brandished the makeshift spear toward the beast.

The beast slowed its approach, eying the weapon.

Kasey took heart. "Yeah, that's what I'm talking about. Take another step and I'll put this clean through you."

The beast cocked its head as if it understood the foolhardy threat. Then it opened its maw and howled in fury, the bellow shaking the house.

Well, that ought to get the neighbors going. All I need to do is survive.

She glanced at the terrifying beast before her. Easier said than done.

The beast lunged forward. Kasey thrusted the lamp spear at its torso. The blow caught the beast in the shoulder, and it recoiled. The beast staggered momentarily but with an angry grunt it resumed its advance. Kasey drew back and thrust again, this time toward what she assumed would be the beast's heart. The wolf caught the weapon in one large clawed fist and stopped it dead. Its other hand reached further down the lamp, then the beast yanked on the makeshift weapon.

Kasey jerked forward, her feet slipping from under her.

Oh crap.

Leaning in, Kasey shoved hard on the lamp rod as she let it go.

The wolf toppled backward, striking the living room floor, taking the lamp with it. Kasey dashed for the front door, leaping over the wolf.

It reached up with one clawed fist and caught her foot. She slammed to the ground, driving the air from her lungs.

As Kasey struggled to catch her breath, the beast rolled over, and rose to its feet. The beast loomed over her. Its open mouth distorted into an almost macabre smile.

The beast raised a clawed fist. Kasey knew how Strode had been killed. His body was only feet from where she now lay. Her gaze played slowly over each razor-sharp claw.

Desperate and alone, Kasey drew on the one hope she had left. Her magic. Screw the Arcane Council.

She started to conjure a fireball.

A knock at the front door interrupted her incantation. The beast's head snapped around as it looked toward the door.

Kasey scowled, uncertain what to do. The beast's eyes darted around. Clearly, it had not planned on being discovered, and the situation was quickly spiraling out of control.

In one sweeping gesture, the beast caught Kasey by the windbreaker and lifted her into the air.

Kasey refocused her thoughts, seeking to slay the beast with a devastating arcane assault.

But before she could mutter a word, the wolf turned and hurled her straight through the living room's large bay window.

CHAPTER 10

Kasey's world slowed to a crawl as she struck the window. Glass exploded outward as she smashed through the thin pane. Kasey winced as the glass sliced into her arms and face.

Pain shot through her body as she lost momentum and began to fall, landing heavily in the garden. The impact of the ground drove the air from her lungs.

The beast, where is it?

Kasey tried to stand but the garden's foliage rubbed against her fresh wounds, intensifying her agony. Clutching her hand against her chest she fought to regain her breath.

"Ow." She gritted her teeth against the pain of her sweat trickling into the myriad of cuts caused by the broken window.

The pain threatened to paralyze her, but Kasey wanted to place as much distance between herself and the wolf-creature as possible. Mustering the last of her energy Kasey rolled out of the garden and onto her back.

As her eyes came back into focus, she realized she was not alone. There standing over her was Detective Bishop, gun in hand.

"Kasey, what are you doing here?" Bishop demanded.

"It's...in the house!" Kasey exclaimed, still unable to get to her feet. "Don't let him get away." She wanted to warn Bishop of the beast's nature but didn't want to sound like a lunatic.

Bishop didn't wait. She stalked toward the front door. On finding it locked, she leaned back and kicked the door as hard as she could muster. The door caved and burst inward. Kasey worried as Bishop disappeared into the home, hoping a bullet would be enough to put the beast down.

Still unable to stand, she lay on the lawn in agony, trying to piece together a suitable story for Bishop. After a minute, Bishop re-emerged from the home and holstered her weapon.

"Kasey, he's dead, been dead a while from the look of him. What were you even doing here in the first place?" Bishop strode toward Kasey.

"Following a lead on the car from this morning," Kasey answered.

"What lead?" Bishop asked. "I only got the tip about the stolen car an hour ago."

"Evidence from the scene..." Kasey said, still struggling to catch her breath. "We knew the car was silver so... we searched security footage until we found a silver sedan... Then we ran the plate through the database."

Bishop shook her head.

Kasey struggled off her back, sitting up she continued. "And what do you mean he's dead? I'm not talking about Lincoln, Bishop. I'm talking about the killer. He was in there," Kasey struggled for a suitable description, one that would not sound insane. "He was massive, he couldn't have gone far."

Bishop reached down to help Kasey up.

Kasey took the offered hand only to feel the cold touch of steel as Bishop slid a set of cuffs around her wrist."

"Bishop, what the..." Kasey began.

"You're under arrest, Kasey," Bishop stated. "You have the right to remain silent. Anything you say can, and will, be used against you in a court of law. You have the right to speak to an attorney, and to have an attorney present during questioning. Do you understand your rights as I have explained them?"

"What are you doing, Bishop? You're wasting time," Kasey said, shaking the cuffs. "What are these? I'm on your side."

"On my side?" Bishop asked. "And what side would that be? You show up here, out of the blue with a dead body and a story so leaky it could be a colander. What do you expect me to do? You're staying in those cuffs until I work out what on earth is going on here."

Kasey lost it. "We are so close, for crying out loud! The killer was in there only moments ago. He threw me through the window, did you not see that? Do you think that I threw myself through the window?"

"Well, now that you mention it, you could well have leaped through the window. There was certainly no sign of anyone else in the house, other than that body, and he certainly isn't in any shape to throw you through a window."

Kasey shook her head in frustration. "I didn't even know it was you out here, so why would I throw myself through a window when it could have been anyone waiting here? If I was guilty, wouldn't I have just legged it out the back door like the killer did?"

"I don't know, Kasey. You've been acting increasingly erratic these last few days. I don't know what you would have done, or why you are even here. But we will get to the bottom of it, and we'll be doing it at the station. Backup is on the way. As soon as they secure the scene, we're out of here," Bishop said.

The sound of sirens in the distance grew nearer.

"Erratic, Bishop? It seems to have escaped your attention, but someone is roaming the city killing women that look like me. I'm sorry if I appear a little on edge." Sarcasm dripped from every word.

She shook her head. By the time she got through to Bishop, the killer would be long gone. How was she going to explain the hulking wolf creature to the NYPD? She would sound like she had lost her mind.

Changing tact, she implored Bishop. "Fine, Bishop, take me down to the station but first, please go inside and grab the folders. They are scattered around the living room. I was trying to get out of the house when the killer confronted me. The folders contain detailed profiles of all the victims. Beth, Brandy, they are both there, but more importantly there are a stack of others, as well. There must be close to twenty. If you are going to drag me down to the station, at least bring those so that we have something useful to talk about. The psychopath has plans for other women, Bishop. The two we've seen so far are just a drop in the bucket. Even now, the others are in danger."

Bishop looked from Kasey to the house and then back to Kasey. "Fine, but not until you're in the back seat. I'm not chasing you through suburbia if you decide to do a runner."

Kasey made a sound of protest as she dragged herself to her feet. "Let's go. Toss me in the car and get back in the house. We need those folders, and those girls need us. I almost died today. The least you can do is make sure we get the evidence I found."

"Suit yourself." Bishop grabbed Kasey by the arm, leading her to the squad car. She opened the door and gestured to the back seat. "Mind your head," she muttered as she pushed Kasey into the car.

Kasey seethed but held her tongue. Bishop was stubborn. The harder Kasey fought, the more Bishop would dig in. Kasey needed the evidence to vindicate her. Strode had been dead for days and Kasey had a solid alibi. She had spent most of that time with Bishop and the rest of it in the station. The real question was how much damage the killer would do in the meantime.

Bishop disappeared back into the house, and Kasey weighed her options.

Part of her considered blasting through the handcuffs and escaping but she knew in her heart how that would end. The NYPD would focus its efforts on finding her rather than the killer and the beast would be left to roam free. Who knew how many more lives would be lost?

She sat still, biding her time as another squad car rolled up. The officers flashed Kasey a confused look as they headed into the house. Bishop emerged moments later, her hands bulging with papers and folders. She dumped the paperwork on the front seat and then climbed into the driver side.

Fastening her seatbelt, she turned to Kasey. "I just had another look at that body, Kasey. We are going down to the station and you are going to tell me exactly what happened in there."

She turned and started the car.

I don't think I can do that.

She was still trying to piece together what had happened herself.

***

Kasey sat in the same chair Brad had occupied the day before, her fingers pounding a rhythmic beat into the steel table of the interrogation room. Without her phone, it was difficult to tell just how long she had been sitting here. She knew at least an hour had lapsed.

Somewhere out there, a killer was targeting young women. The fact that those young women all bore more than a passing resemblance to herself had nagged her from the moment Vida had drawn her attention to it. Her own attack had her on edge. Was she a target? Why were wizards and werewolves combing the streets of New York killing innocent women? Were they working together or was it simply happenstance?

Doubtless the folders she had found were the key to this mystery, and every minute wasted in this room was time that would have been better spent studying their contents.

For the thousandth time she wished she'd had the time to read them all.

After an eternity, the door opened, and Bishop entered, accompanied by Vida. Bishop carried with her the pile of manila folders, though now they were far more ordered than the jumbled mess she had tossed on the front seat of the squad car.

She placed the folders in the center of the table and quietly made her way around the table to reach Kasey. "Sorry about the cuffs, Kasey, but you have to admit, finding you at the scene like that didn't give me a lot of choices."

"I don't know, Bishop, you could have tried listening to me," Kasey replied, more than a little annoyed.

Bishop reached over and unlocked the cuffs. "Well, next time you are going to try to track down a serial killer all on your own, perhaps you'll think it out a little further and give your partner the courtesy of a heads up."

Kasey rubbed her newly freed wrists. "Does this mean I'm no longer a suspect?"

"Indeed, it does," Bishop replied. "Vida's inspection of the body showed that he's been dead for days. Likely killed by whoever stole his car and used it to run down Brandy. At the time in question, you and I were here in the station interrogating Brad. You couldn't have done it."

"Thanks for the vote of confidence, Bishop. I would have preferred, 'of course not, Kasey, we know you're not a murdering psychopath.' I mean, you have spent the better part of two weeks working side-by-side with me. I would have thought you'd figured out at least that much."

"Sure, that too," Bishop replied unconvincingly. "Now if we can get past everyone's hurt feelings, we have a case to solve. Vida mentioned your earlier theory about a serial killer. I wish you had said something sooner. We could have begun comparing and analyzing the victims to work out the killers M.O. Fortunately for us, you stumbled onto a gold mine, Kasey." She tapped the folders in front of her. "Most serial killers aren't dumb enough to document their targets and leave them lying around for us to find."

"I don't think he was expecting us to show up when we did," Kasey replied. "I think I took him by surprise. After reporting Strode's car as stolen, he probably thought he had more than a few hours to relocate. It seems like he's been using Lincoln's house as his base of operations."

"Yes, it does, which in and of itself is quite strange. Most serial killers operate from a place of comfort, like their own home. Yet this one stays on the move, using Strode's home and car instead of his own. It's unconventional, to say the least. Normally, I would think he is acting erratically, but all evidence is to the contrary. We haven't caught him on a single camera, neither has he left any meaningful evidence at any of the scenes. Instead, he has carried out his killings with clinical efficiency. This man is dangerous, and you're the only one who's even seen him. What did he look like?"

There was no way of explaining the werewolf to two normals, so Kasey shook her head as she tried to muster a convincing lie. "Sorry, Bishop, but I'm not going to be a whole lot of help there. The guy got the drop on me and was wearing a balaclava. I can tell you he was massive though, well over seven foot, maybe as tall as seven foot six. We tussled and I tried to get a better look at his face, but I got thrown through the window for my troubles."

"You're lucky he didn't kill you," Bishop replied.

"I think he was too busy trying to escape to worry about me," Kasey answered. "He only took an interest in me after he saw me with those folders. They're loaded with information about his victims. It's like he's been stalking them for weeks."

"We know, Kasey. We've been through them... that's why we are surprised you're still alive."

"Still alive? I don't get it," Kasey said.

Bishop and Vida exchanged nervous glances.

Bishop drew the topmost folder off the pile and slid it across the table in front of Kasey. "We thought you knew... You're in the folder."

Kasey ripped the folder off the table and flicked it open. There staring back at her was a picture of herself. It had her current name, date of birth, and study history ending with NYU. It outlined her employment with the OCME and her transfer to the NYPD. It also had an extensive background on her family. Her parents were listed, along with her sister.

Kasey felt violated. The creep had been following her for weeks, maybe months.

Vida was first to break the awkward silence. "I know we joked about it before, Kasey, but it is no joke now. This man is hunting you. You could have been killed."

"All the more reason for us to find him," Kasey bit back. "We need to find him before he kills anyone else. Me being in this pile changes nothing." She tried putting on a brave face, but the realization had shaken her to her core. "There are more than a dozen other women at risk here. At least I know what's coming my way. These other women have no idea..."

"The department will take care of them, Kasey," Bishop replied. "We need to keep you safe."

"Well, I don't think I could be much safer than I am here," Kasey said. "I doubt he's going to tackle the entirety of the Fighting Ninth just to get to me. Besides, I am the only person who has seen him. I'm far more useful with you than I am cooped up at home. You need me and I need to be here."

"Fine," Bishop relented. "But no more running around on your own. You'll get yourself killed."

"I can live with that," Kasey replied. "Where do we start?"

"We start with these folders. We need to know what else links all these women together. We know they look similar, but there must be something more, otherwise we'd have hundreds of folders, not twenty. If we can find what that something is, we can cut him off at the pass," Bishop replied spreading the folders out on the table.

"Any ideas?" Kasey asked. "It seems like you've been through them once already."

"Not particularly," Bishop responded, a little defeated. "They are all in their late 20's, all of them are between five-five and six-two. All of them live in New York City or its surrounds. Other than that, I am struggling to draw any common threads between them. They aren't related and as far as I can tell there is no overlap in dating history. So, we aren't dealing with a crazy ex-boyfriend."

"The fact that all the victims are women does indicate a bias in his profiling," Vida began. "Maybe he was rejected by a lover and is taking it out on anyone he can find who bears a passing resemblance to her."

"Perhaps," Bishop replied. "I've certainly seen weirder things over the years. But those kinds of serial killers normally follow a pattern, with each victim killed in a similar manner. So far, our killer has struck twice, and both scenes were completely different. We wouldn't have even linked the two if it hadn't been for Kasey finding these folders. These murders were clean and calculated. This man is dangerous, and we need to tread carefully."

The three pored over the folders as they searched for answers.

After an hour, Bishop threw her folder on the table in disgust. "I know there is more to this we aren't seeing. But for the life of me I can't find it. It's so irritating, together in a pool these women are obviously similar. Similar in height, weight, age, and appearance. But you take any two of them and that is where it ends. They don't work together, date the same people, or even share the same hobbies. It makes no sense."

"That's because there is none," Vida replied. "On their own, they appear random and together they have only the faintest semblance of a connection. He's not trying to kill every twenty-something year old brunette in New York. He's singled out these women for a reason. I think our killer is looking for someone or something and these folders are just his attempt to narrow the field."

"I guess it's something and that's good news," Kasey answered.

"Yes and no," Vida replied. "If he doesn't find what he's looking for, he may just widen the net. If we don't find him, there is no telling how far he'll go."

"Well, we know who he's after," Kasey said. "If we follow these women, he's bound to show up eventually."

"We can't use them as bait, Kasey." Bishop pinched the bridge of her nose. "Besides, we've already dispatched officers to round up as many as we can."

There was a knock at the door.

"Come in," Bishop called.

The door opened and an officer's head appeared through the crack. The officer was a few years younger than Kasey.

"What's up, Stevens?" Bishop asked as she resumed studying the folders before her.

"We are working with other precincts across the city to round up these women, detective. We have most of them in our care. Of the potential victims living in our borough, we have all but one."

"Who's missing?" Bishop asked.

"Trudie Sears. She wasn't home when we stopped by her apartment. Apparently, she works at a bar in Brooklyn. The Drift. We have officers heading there now..."

Kasey's chair ground against the floor as she shot out of it. "Bishop, we've got to go."

"Go where, Kasey?"

"There!" Kasey exclaimed. "The Drift. When I first searched through the folders, Trudie's was third, right after Beth and Brandy. If our killer is working in order, Trudie is next on his list."

Bishop leaped to her feet. "Stevens, get on dispatch now. Warn those officers that they are about to have company. Have them hold tight. We're on our way."

CHAPTER 11

Kasey did her best to ignore the blaring sirens as the squad car made its way over the Williamsburg Bridge. Bishop took no prisoners as she tore through Brooklyn. Even at this late hour, there was traffic but with the lights and sirens helping to clear a path, they reached the Brooklyn Queens Expressway in record time.

A burst of static issued from the radio. "Bishop, this is Henley, we are en route to The Drift but there has been an accident on Queens Boulevard. We are at a standstill."

Bishop grabbed the radio with one hand and pressed the transmit button. "Henley, Bishop here. We are en route from the precinct and are only minutes away. Are you sure she's working tonight?"

"Affirmative. Building super spoke with her on the way out. Started her shift at six, and works till the early hours," Henley replied.

"Well get here as soon as you can. We have reason to believe the killer may be in the area. We could use the backup."

"Understood, Bishop. We'll be there as soon as we can," Henley answered.

Bishop slammed down the radio. "It's you and me, Kasey."

"You keep driving like this, Bishop, and Trudie is going to be on her own," Kasey replied, gripping her seat as Bishop made the U-turn under the Brooklyn Queens Expressway.

"Don't pansy out on me now, Kasey. That's The Drift there on the right," Bishop replied casually. "Are you ready to go another round with this guy?"

Kasey winced at the thought. She was still sore from the afternoon's encounter, but more importantly she had no way of preparing Bishop for the beast she'd faced on Hudson Road.

"I still feel like I got hit by a bus, Bishop, so do me a favor. You see this guy making a move, put a bullet in him and make our lives a lot easier."

"Ha-ha, Kasey, very funny. There is such a thing as excessive force."

"He put me through a window, Bishop." Kasey labored each word for emphasis, "Trust me when I say, a bullet is exactly the right amount of force."

Bishop didn't answer as she screeched the squad car to an abrupt halt outside of The Drift. She killed the sirens but left the lights running.

Kasey leaped out of the car, anxious to reach Trudie before it was too late. Together with Bishop she made her way into the bar.

The dive bar featured a skiing theme with an assortment of hunting trophies lining the walls. Kasey wasn't a fan, but Brooklyn was. The tiny bar was packed with patrons and it was difficult to move freely due to the throng of guests. Kasey and Bishop pressed their way through the crowd. There were protestations but one look at Bishop's badge and stern demeanor, and they beat a hasty retreat.

Kasey searched for Trudie. The picture in her folder had showed a young woman in her twenties. In the photo, she'd been wearing a t-shirt with cut out jeans, and carrying an instrument case, likely a guitar from the size and shape of it. Kasey wasn't expecting Trudie to be in the same clothes, but as a barkeeper in a dive bar it was likely that she'd be similarly attired.

She didn't find any sign of her. The only person behind the bar was a young man. The bartender was handsome. If Kasey weren't in such a hurry, her gaze would certainly have lingered a little longer. His tight black t-shirt did little to hide his well-chiseled form, and his biceps looked like they should have had separate post-codes. Kasey tried to clear her mind and focus on the task at hand.

Fortunately, Bishop was on point.

Bishop made her way straight over to the bar. Leaning over the wooden counter, she edged out a young woman who was locked in conversation with the bartender.

"Hey," the young woman cried, scowling.

Bishop simply held up her badge and didn't give the woman a second glance. "You, there." She pointed at the bartender. "I'm looking for Trudie. Is she on tonight?"

The young man took one glance at Bishop and a second look at the badge before replying. "Why? What's she done?"

"Nothing at all," Bishop replied, leaning over the counter until her face was less than a foot from the bartender. "But we have reason to believe her life is in danger. If you know where she is, spill it now. Anything happens to her and we will be coming back for you."

The man backed away, raising both hands in self-defense. "Whoa, easy there, officer. Just looking out for a friend. You know how it is. Trudie is out back, just emptying the trash. Should be back any minute."

Bishop and Kasey exchanged worried glances.

"Which way to the back?" Bishop demanded.

"Quickest way is through the kitchen, just through those doors there." The bartender pointed at a set of silver doors off to the right.

Kasey and Bishop rounded the bar and burst into the kitchen. The space was small but busy, three cooks fussed over the food preparation for the packed bar. Between the cooks, the waitstaff and an industrial dishwasher that was rattling away, it was difficult to hear a word.

The chef closest to the door whirled around to face them, but Bishop was already on top of him with her badge. "NYPD. Just passing through."

He scowled, then went back to the dish he was carefully plating up.

Kasey spotted a door at the kitchen's rear.

"Is the trash through there?" she asked, almost shouting to be heard over the commotion.

The chef toiling away at the grill nodded. "Yeah, just some trash and an alleyway. Why?"

Kasey ignored the question as Bishop beelined for the door. Throwing it open, Bishop and Kasey spilled into the alleyway. It was dark and narrow, the lights from the expressway blocked by the apartments over the bar.

An overhead bulb illuminated a few feet around the door, but for the most part the alley was hidden in shadow.

Oh, no, we're too late.

"Spread out and search for her," Bishop called. "I'll head right, you go left."

Kasey nodded as her eyes struggled to adapt and began cautiously moving down the alleyway, searching for any sign of Trudie. Images of Beth lying in the alleyway came surging back into Kasey's mind. She tried to push them out but soon the beast dominated her thoughts. In her mind's eye, she could see its snarling maw laden with razor sharp teeth. Its red eyes locked on hers.

It had been bad enough at Hudson Road, at least the home had lights. Finding the beast here in the darkness of the alley would be terrifying.

Her pulse quickened just thinking about it. Rather than fumbling about in the dark, she pulled out her smart phone and flicked on the light. The bright LED illuminated the alleyway, providing a little reassurance.

As Kasey made her way down the alley, she spotted something sticking out from behind a dumpster. Moving closer Kasey found a pair of legs, protruding from a sprawling pile of refuse.

"Trudie!" Kasey shouted as she edged toward the body. Reaching the pile of trash, she swept the light over it, focusing on the body lying among it.

As the face came into view, Kasey found herself staring down at a disheveled man in his fifties. The man was wearing a pair of old jeans and a tattered New York Yankees hoodie. A scraggly beard covered most of his face, the brown hairs given way to gray. It had been years since the man had seen a razor.

The homeless man was not what she had expected. She leaned in to check his pulse and instantly regretted it. The smell of stale beer and garbage hit her like a wave.

The man lurched to life before opening both eyes. Kasey leaped back a mile. The man flailed his arms around, as if trying to drive back the blinding light from the phone.

Kasey backed away but tripped over another bag of garbage. She landed on her butt as her cell phone skittered across the ground.

"I see you've met Steve," an unfamiliar voice said, "but why are you looking for me?"

Kasey startled and found a woman standing over her. lit cigarette in hand, and an amused grin stretching from ear to ear.

"Trudie?" Kasey asked hopefully, ignoring her embarrassing display of clumsiness.

"Who's asking?" The woman took a long draw on her cigarette.

Kasey grabbed her cell and struggled to her feet. "I'm Kasey Chase with the NYPD. We have reason to believe your life is in danger."

She looked from the woman to the cigarette she was smoking and couldn't help but appreciate the irony.

"Danger, huh? Well, your presence fills me with confidence, Officer Chase."

The sarcasm hit a nerve and for a moment, Kasey considered leaving. The thought of the beast catching up with the little brat was almost tempting.

Footsteps drew Kasey's attention and she turned to see Bishop hurrying up the alley toward them. Bishop had her gun in hand as she searched for the source of the noise.

"I'm no officer, but she is," Kasey replied, pointing to Bishop, "and as I said, we are here to help you. If you don't want that help, that's fine. Keep being a smart-ass and we'll leave you here."

"What's wrong with here? And why would I need your help?" Trudie replied.

"Miss Sears," Bishop said, stepping forward. "We are hunting a serial killer who is operating in the greater New York area. So far, we have two women in the morgue, and we have reason to believe you might be next. We need you to come down to the station for safekeeping."

"Station? If I leave in the middle of my shift, I'll be sacked," Trudie said, turning for the kitchen.

Bishop caught her arm. "I'll deal with your boss, Trudie. Trust me when I say there are worse things in life than being fired. Being dead is certainly one of them. Now come with us so we can get out of this alley."

"Fine." Trudie dropped her cigarette, and then stepped on the still smoldering butt and ground it against the pavement. "Let's go."

Bishop stared at the discarded cigarette butt. "We'll go, all right, but first you'll be picking that up. You might be determined to kill yourself, but others share this city too, so learn to clean up after yourself."

"Are you kidding me?" Trudie replied. "You're talking about a serial killer hunting me and you're worried about a lousy cigarette butt."

"The sooner you toss it in the trash, the sooner we can get out of here," Bishop replied impassively.

Trudie shook her fist but picked up the butt regardless. Tossing it in the trash, she turned to Bishop. "Happy now?"

"Quite," Bishop replied. Kasey could have sworn she saw the corners of Bishop's mouth peaking upwards into a smile as she steered Trudie forward. "We aren't going back through the bar. It's too crowded. We'll head around. Once we're out of the alley, it's a clear run to the car. We'll be out of here in no time."

Kasey followed them as they headed down the alleyway toward the street. She opened her mouth to say something but stopped.

A hulking black shape appeared from the street, cutting off their escape.

CHAPTER 12

Kasey stopped dead. The silhouette at the alley's entrance caused her heart to leap into her throat.

With one hand, Bishop shoved Trudie toward Kasey. With the other, she drew her compact Glock 19 from its holster on her hip.

"Stop right there!" Bishop demanded. "Put your hands in the air."

The silhouette responded by raising both of its immense arms.

Kasey glanced at Trudie. The bartender was staring slack jawed at the shape in the mouth of the alley. Not taking any chances, Kasey raised one of her hands, concealed from view by a dumpster, and began conjuring a fireball.

"Pêl Tân," she whispered as wisps of flame began to swirl and form above her outstretched palm. Arcane Council or not, she wasn't going to let the beast manhandle her again. She'd set it ablaze and deal with the consequences as they came.

"Bishop..." A voice called from the alley's entrance. It sounded distinctly like it was coming from the hulking beast.

Bishop sighed audibly. "Henley, what are you doing? Why are you creeping around in the dark?"

Kasey's shoulders slumped in relief. She snapped her fist shut, and the flames vanished.

"Providing backup," he replied. "We saw your car out front. Morales is in the bar. I circled around to check the perimeter. Can I put my hands down yet?"

"Of course. Use your flashlight next time."

"Will do, detective." He lowered his arms.

At seven-foot-three, Josiah Henley was one of the largest officers in the Ninth Precinct. Once a linebacker with a college scholarship to Arizona State, Henley had been compared favorably to a freight-train hitting at speed. Following the unexpected death of his parents in a home invasion, Henley had withdrawn from college and moved home to care for his younger brother and sister who were still at school. The Academy had turned the linebacker into a lawman and the Fighting Ninth had won out as the rookie's first posting.

As her pulse eased back to normal, Kasey reached out to Trudie. "Are you okay?"

Trudie shook her head, white as a sheet. Clearly, the scare from Henley's sudden appearance had caused her to think twice about her nonchalance in the face of danger. She was shaking.

So, she should be. At least we won't have to tell her twice to keep her head down now.

Bishop took charge. "Henley, we need to get Trudie and Chase out of here and back to the station. I'm going to need you to take point, clear the way to the vehicle. If you see anything suspicious, drop it like it's hot. We're dealing with a murderer, so stay on your toes."

Kasey followed Henley as he led the way out of the alley. Bishop's gun never made it back to the holster. Even the Detective's iron nerves were starting to fray.

Her wariness proved unnecessary and the group arrived safely at the squad cars.

Kasey opened the door for Trudie and helped her into the backseat. If she had any reservations about riding in the rear, she didn't voice them. In fact, Trudie hadn't said a word since Henley had appeared in the alley.

"Henley, fetch Morales and meet us back at the station," Bishop said as she slid behind the steering wheel. "We're going to need all hands on deck to keep these women safe."

"Understood, detective. We'll see you back at the station," he replied, then turned back for The Drift.

Kasey slumped into the passenger seat. The fatigue of the past twenty-four hours weighing her down. She had to fight just to keep her eyes open as they hit the Brooklyn Queen's Expressway, heading for the safety of the Ninth Precinct.

As the squad car pulled into the station, Kasey turned to Bishop. "Can you take it from here? After last night, I need to sleep. I'm drifting off here in the seat. What I really need is a good night's sleep in my own bed."

Bishop pulled into her parking space before answering. "I hate to be the bearer of bad news, Kasey, but you aren't going home. The killer is still out there, and he knows where you live. With all the other targets in custody, you'll be the only one left for him to go after. It's crazy and I won't have it. If it's sleep you need, you can bed down in the station, but you aren't going home. At least not tonight, not until we have a better handle on what is going on."

Kasey's head fell back against the headrest. She knew what Bishop was saying made sense, but she was exhausted. The last thing she wanted to do was spend a night on a station couch. "Fine. I guess anywhere is better than where I spent last night."

Bishop smiled. "I know you are angling for an apology, Kasey, but you aren't going to get one. If you'd told me what you were up to, you wouldn't have had to spend the night in cuffs. I'm your partner, or as close as you get to one, so fill me in next time."

Kasey let out a long yawn. "Will do. In the meantime, I'm going to take the couch in the morgue. At least I won't have to fight anyone for that one."

Bishop raised an eyebrow. "You know that's creepy, right? No one likes sleeping in a room full of dead bodies."

Kasey shrugged. "You get used to it. Besides, it's the live ones you've gotta worry about." She popped the door open and dragged herself out of the car. "Night, Bishop."

She shut the door harder than she had intended, then headed toward the station. Slipping through the large double doors, she hit the stairs and made her way down to the morgue. As expected, it was deserted. Vida had long since gone home for the night. Kasey didn't even want to look at her watch but as she flopped onto the faded blue sofa, she made the mistake of glancing at its face.

"Argh, midnight!" she exclaimed, disgusted at how little sleep she'd had over the past few days.

Kicking off her shoes, she stretched out and did her best to clear her mind. There was so much going on, but she wasn't going to be of any use to anyone if she didn't get some rest. Before long, sleep took over.

***

A voice called softly, "Miss Chase."

Kasey ignored it, hoping the unwelcome disturbance would depart.

Instead, Kasey felt something shaking her foot. She reluctantly opened one eye to see Kathleen, Chief West's personal assistant, standing over her.

"Ah, Miss Chase. I'm sorry to have to wake you, but the chief wishes to see you. It really cannot wait." Kathleen smiled apologetically.

Kasey sighed and struggled off the couch. The sleep had helped but she still felt like she'd been run over by a freight train. A dull headache pounded at the base of her skull while the sting of a dozen cuts and bruises, reminded her of her involuntary trip through the window at Hudson Road.

"I'll just be a minute, Kathleen," she answered as she made her way into the bathroom.

A glance in the mirror took her by surprise. The myriad of cuts on her face had all been cleaned and dressed.

Clearly Bishop or Vida had taken pity on her and cleaned her up. In her catatonic state, she hadn't even noticed. A cut on her left arm had also been treated and dressed. The bruise on her jaw was starting to fade though black bags were forming under her eyes from her steady pattern of sleep deprivation.

I'm a train wreck. I need some help.

She pulled out her phone from her pocket, then hastily punched out a text. Tucking the phone back in her pocket, she turned on the tap and splashed some water on her face to try and wake herself up a little more. The water stung as it contacted her wounds, but she welcomed it. The niggling pain dragged her back to reality.

She freshened up as best she could but found herself wishing she'd left a brush in the office. Her bag was still in her car and it didn't seem like Kathleen was going to wait forever, so she called it quits and headed back to the morgue. Kathleen was still standing by the couch.

"Lead the way," Kasey said.

Kathleen examined Kasey. "Are you ok, Miss Chase? You look like you've had a rough night."

"More of a rough week, Kathleen, but I'll pull through."

"Can I get you anything? A stick of gum, a hairbrush. Anything?"

"A brush would be a lifesaver. I feel like a pigeon has made its home in my hair. The whole thing is a tangled mess."

"Sure do. I never leave home without it," Kathleen replied, reaching into her handbag before handing a small brush to Kasey.

"Kathleen, you're my hero." Kasey took the offered brush and disappeared back into the bathroom. Using the mirror, she wrestled her hair into submission and returned it to some semblance of normality. "Much better," she told herself as she examined her reflection. Back in the morgue, she handed the brush back to Kathleen. "Thanks, Kathleen, I truly appreciate it. It's the little things that make a difference, you know? Are you good to go?"

"Sorry, Kasey I have to run another errand for the chief, but if you head up to the fourth floor, he's expecting you."

"Alright, Kathleen. Thanks again," Kasey replied as she headed for the elevator. She took it up to the fourth floor.

What was Chief West after? Would this be another warning? After all, she had been discovered at a murder scene and spent the night in interrogation with Bishop. She may have come up clean, but she had a suspicion that might not matter to the chief.

Or did this meeting have something to do with the rapidly spiraling murder case that was now tying up considerable station resources? Serial killers tended to attract negative press, their reign of terror highlighting the police's inability to bring them to justice.

As of the moment, there were no actionable leads on the case. The sum total of the evidence they had collected may have detailed the victims at great length, but they provided little of value on the killer himself.

Kasey still struggled to understand the beast she had faced at Hudson Road. She had wanted to tell Bishop about the encounter, but every time she played over the words in her head, she sounded entirely crazy. Better to let Bishop see the beast for herself.

At least then Bishop won't try to have me admitted.

Her mind turned to the victims. With two in the morgue and almost twenty women under guard in precincts across the city, the case had grown far beyond what Kasey had anticipated.

The werewolf had killed Beth. The hair she had found at the scene had matched the beast she had faced at Hudson Road. His presence there also made him the most likely suspect in Brandy's murder; after all it was Strode's car that had been used.

Who was the wizard then? Was he working with the werewolf? Or were there two different deadly individuals hunting her?

Staring at her profile in the folder had been a surreal experience. She had searched her memory for someone who would have the motive to want her dead but kept coming up blank. There was always John Ainsley who was still nursing his broken ribs, but it didn't make sense. If it was truly John, wanting her dead, why target the other women?

Was it some bizarre mind game designed to torment her? If it was, it was working. The Ainsley angle made little sense, though. Sure, they were rich but murder for a few broken ribs? That was a stretch.

The elevator chimed as the doors opened. Kasey made her way across the waiting room to Chief West's office. The door was open, but she stopped nonetheless.

Mirroring Kathleen's earlier approach, she knocked on the glass. "Chief West. Kathleen told me you wished to see me."

"Ah, Kasey, come on in." Chief West motioned to the two chairs in front of his desk.

A man already sat in the second chair. As Kasey entered the room, the man stood to meet her. He wore an expensive Italian suit, its pinstripe exaggerating his already considerable height. At a glance, he appeared to be in his forties but on closer inspection, Kasey could see the gray roots in among his dyed blond hair. She supposed him to be in his late fifties.

The man extended his hand as he greeted her. "Kasey, it's a pleasure to meet you. I've heard so much about you."

Kasey eyed the expensive suit and the man who wore it with skepticism and suspicion. "And yet I've heard nothing about you."

She shook his hand.

"Let me remedy that. My name is Arthur Ainsley."

Kasey deflated. That could only mean...

"Yes. That's right, I'm John's father," the man replied, clearly enjoying the effect his announcement had had on her.

She took one look at the man's smile and shook her head. She liked him just as much as she liked his son. The smile had all the authenticity of a politician.

Her displeasure must've been visible as Arthur released her hand and said, "Oh, come now, Kasey, I know you've had your disagreements with my son, but rest assured he has been dealt with. As soon as I learned what transpired, I put an end to it. I'm here in good faith, responding to the earnest outreach of Chief West, a man for whom I have the greatest respect."

"Arthur, there is no need for such flagrant flattery," the chief replied. "I appreciate you coming down here as I want to get to the bottom of this. Please, both of you, take a seat."

Kasey sat down but immediately twisted to face Arthur. "What do you mean, when you found out? You've known for weeks. Your family practically drove me out of the OCME. You've made my life miserable."

Arthur Ainsley raised both of his hands defensively. "Don't confuse me with my son, or his actions. As far as I'm concerned, he was way out of line when he harassed you and has paid the price for his poor choice. I'll not do my son the disservice of shielding him from the consequences of his actions.

"When I learned he was using our family's influence to inflict his revenge, I put a stop to it. Believe it or not, I had no idea anything had transpired until Chief West called me. John isn't proud of the fact you beat him six ways from Sunday. He certainly wasn't going to come cry to me about it."

Kasey bristled as she weighed the man who sat beside her. His demeanor couldn't be more different than that of his son.

Chief West filled the awkward silence. "As I said before, Arthur, I appreciate you coming down here. Like I said on the phone, with the current situation continuing to develop, I didn't want John's vendetta dragging your family's name through the mud."

"I appreciate it, chief. I give my assurance that John has nothing to do with what is happening to these young women. It is simply an unfortunate coincidence that Miss Chase with whom he has a grudge, is caught up in the case herself. He will cease any and all action against Miss Chase, and we will lend our considerable resources to ensure the killer is brought to justice. If there is anything you need, simply name it."

"I appreciate the thought, Arthur, but for the time being the Fighting Ninth is well equipped to deal with the task at hand. All I ask is that John give Kasey a wide berth so that we can keep her safe."

"Consider it done," Arthur replied.

Chief West turned his attention to Kasey. "And you, Miss Chase. You will remain on secondment to the Fighting Ninth until this serial killer has been caught. You are far safer here than you are at the OCME. When we have the killer in custody, you will be free to return to your previous station should you so choose. Do you have any questions?"

The reference to her old job took Kasey off-balance. The OCME felt like it was a lifetime ago, and as hectic as working at the precinct was, she enjoyed being in the field. It felt like she was making a difference every day.

Kasey shook her head. "No, chief, none from me."

"Very well, you're excused. Stay close to Bishop until this is resolved."

Kasey nodded and rose out of the chair. Without further word, she slipped quietly out of the chief's office and made her way to the elevator. Despite all that was happening, she felt somehow lighter. With the threat of John Ainsley behind her, she was finally moving forward with her life.

She mashed the call button on the elevator, and tapped her foot as she waited, eyes glued on the elevator's floor readout.

An immense shadow appeared across the elevator doors.

Spinning around, she found Arthur Ainsley standing behind her. At over seven feet tall, he cast an impressive shadow.

Kasey tried not to register her surprise but failed miserably. In the wake of the last few days, her nerves were frayed and she was far more jumpy than usual.

"Easy there, Arthur. The last Ainsley to sneak up on me like that was nursing a set of broken ribs moments later."

Arthur smiled. "Fair point, Miss Chase. I'll keep that in mind." He paused. Clearly, there was something he wished to say but he was taking his time.

The elevator dinged, and Kasey stepped through the opening doors.

"You know, Miss Chase, for a woman of your gifts, I'm surprised a few broken ribs was the extent of it," Arthur Ainsley said as he joined her in the elevator.

Kasey eyed him. "Look, I'm going to be honest. If I knew the trouble he was going to cause me, I'd have probably hit him a few more times just for good measure."

She chuckled at the thought and pressed the button for the ground floor.

"Yes, precisely my point," Arthur said. "After your brush with the ADI, I'm surprised you didn't reduce him to cinders or blow him through a wall."

Her heart stopped.

"How do you..." She caught herself just in time. "I don't know what you're talking about."

"Oh, yes you do, Miss Chase. Your little exhibition the other night. It took the ADI hours just to clean up the mess. What I can't work out, is why you didn't do the same to John when you had the chance?"

Kasey just stood there mute. What did Arthur Ainsley know about the ADI? Was there anything money couldn't buy?

"Oh... You didn't know..." Arthur laughed heartily. "A witch and a wizard right under each other's noses and neither of you even knew. That is hilarious."

If Kasey had felt relief earlier, Arthur's revelation smashed it to pieces.

"You're wizards..." Kasey began. "I should have known. The ADI and their visit. That was you. You have friends on the Arcane Council.

Arthur's smile disappeared as he loomed over her. "No, Miss Chase. I am the Arcane Council."

CHAPTER 13

K asey stood, staring down the imposing figure of Arthur Ainsley.

The elevator shuddered to life, but Arthur swept a hand across the control panel.

"Forfyllan," he muttered. His voice was quiet yet unyielding. The language was foreign to Kasey, but its impact was clear. The elevator ground to a halt.

"Now, you listen to me, and you listen well, Miss Chase. When it comes to the Council, my voice is the only one that matters."

"I don't care about your council, Arthur," Kasey retorted. "If I did, I would have registered. I want you, your son, and your Council out of my way, and out of my life!"

Arthur's face creased with anger as he pointed at her. "Listen, you ungrateful little wretch, it doesn't matter what you want. The Council governs all arcane matters in the Unites States. When a young witch uses her powers like a vigilante to hunt down criminals, those matters come across my desk. I was lenient once. But you should understand that there is a limit. The next time your name crosses my desk, and I think we both know that it will, you may not be so fortunate."

"So, what is it you want, Arthur? You didn't come down here for that farce upstairs. You could have sent your goons. You want something. Something you couldn't ask for in front of the Chief. What is it?"

Arthur composed himself. "Very perceptive, Miss Chase. This case you're working, I think we both know your suspect is no ordinary killer."

"I can't disclose the details of an active investigation," Kasey replied. "But as you heard from Chief West, we do suspect he is a serial killer, with all that entails."

"That is not what I'm referring to, Miss Chase. Don't play dumb with me. He's a Werewolf. That particular detail could not have escaped your attention."

"Wait, how could you know that?" Kasey demanded, her mind racing as she thought of the beast she had faced at Hudson Road.

"Because we have the hair sample your boss submitted to the FBI. When it didn't register a match in the NYPD's database, he called in the cavalry. Fortunately, we made it disappear before it could cause too much of a stir."

"Why would you do that? That was the one piece of evidence we had on him."

"Evidence, Miss Chase? What do you need the evidence for? To find him? Or convict him? Because if it is the former, let me help you. We've already analyzed the sample and determined that it belongs to Danilo Lelac, a Hungarian assassin of some repute. If it is the latter, I would advise you to wake up. There won't be a trial for a Werewolf in central New York City. There will be no jail for Danilo Lelac. If you find him, you are to kill him."

"What? I can't do that. If you haven't noticed, I have half the NYPD in tow thanks to this Danilo. How am I meant to find him, let alone kill him, without the NYPD getting wind of it?"

"That, Kasey, would be your problem. I'm sure you'll work it out. If not...well, best not to consider such unpleasantness so early in the day." Arthur reached toward the buttons and muttered another incantation. "Abregdan."

The elevator resumed its downward journey.

"What...But..." she stammered. She was trapped and she knew it. Finding her words at last, she blurted, "Can you be any more help than that? Do you know what he looks like? Anything?"

"I thought you'd seen him, Kasey. He's a damn Werewolf. One of nature's greatest hunters blended with a human form. You won't be able to miss him."

Kasey exhaled audibly. "I don't mean when he's a Wolf. I've seen him in that form. I mean his human form. What does he look like when he's not in his were-form? That would be useful to know."

"Oh, I see," Arthur said. "Unfortunately, we don't know. The Golden Wolf of Hungary, while infamous, is still an unknown. No one who has seen him shift has survived to tell the tale. He is a ghost."

The elevator slowed its descent.

"Does he have any associates? A lanky beady eyed wizard with a penchant for stabbing people to death?" Kasey asked, her brows knit together with concern.

Arthur's eyes widened but he recovered quickly, extending his hand. "The Golden Wolf hunts alone, he's not a wizard, but he's equally as dangerous, Kasey. I wish you the best of luck."

Kasey reluctantly took the offered hand. Antagonizing such a powerful figure in the magical community simply came at too high a price.

As she shook it, a mist descended, clouding her vision. When it dispersed, Kasey was no longer in the elevator. Instead, she was towering over a city. Searching her surroundings, she found herself on the deck of an immense structure. At this height, the cars on the street below were barely visible, miniature ants crawling through the gridlocked city streets. Buildings and skyscrapers stretched as far as her eyes could see.

Kasey knew the skyline... New York City! She'd never seen the city from such a spectacular height. The building she stood on dominated those around it. She could make out the opulent Trump Tower to the west. It was almost miniature in comparison. Below her, Central Park, nature's bastion, built right in the heart of Manhattan. Moving across the deck, Kasey could see clear to the Statue of Liberty. The iconic landmark looked miniature at this distance.

From the majestic vista, Kasey knew she could only be in one building: 432 Park Avenue. The residential tower loomed over the city as one of the tallest residential structures in the world. She had read about the building, but construction wasn't due to complete for several months yet.

This vision is the future.

An explosion in the distance shook her from her reflections. She rushed to the platform's edge, straining her eyes to search the city below.

Thick oily green smoke rose from the streets in a billowing cloud. Another chain of explosions followed. Kasey spun to see the East Village in flames.

The mist descended once more, and Kasey found herself back in the elevator, still clutching Arthur Ainsley's outstretched hand. He raised one eyebrow as he waited for her to relinquish his hand.

"Are you quite alright, Miss Chase?"

Kasey let go. "Ah...I'm sorry. Just feeling a little lightheaded."

"Well, you best get back to work. Our lupine problem won't solve itself."

Kasey nodded. She was still trying to process her vision as Arthur Ainsley stepped out of the elevator and crossed the precinct's lobby.

"Kasey!" a woman shouted.

The voice snapped Kasey from her reflections.

Homing in on the familiar voice, Kasey spotted her sister, Sarah. She was sitting on the black leather lounge of the lobby, bouncing her oldest son, Simeon, on her lap. The three-year-old giggled as he moved.

"Sarah!" Kasey called, racing across the lobby. "You have no idea how good it is to see you."

"Your text had me worried," Sarah replied as she took in Kasey's war wounds. "What on Earth happened to your face? Kasey, what is going on?"

"Can we go somewhere to talk about it?" Kasey asked, desperate to get some fresh air.

"Sure. Have you eaten breakfast yet?"

"No," she said, feeling more and more like a train wreck with each passing moment, "but I could sure go for some. What did you have in mind?"

Sarah paused as she évaluated the options. "There is a cafe a few streets over. We can grab some takeout and head to the park. Can you spare the time out of the office?"

"Spare it. I need it. The job has almost killed me this week." Kasey was tempted to add literally but didn't want to worry her sister. "I'm dying for some breakfast."

"Awesome. Let's go," Sarah replied as she stood up. Catching Kasey's eye, she smiled. "Want to hold Simeon?"

Kasey looked longingly at her nephew. The adorable little one shared his mother's sandy hair and easy smile. It made Kasey's heart melt.

"Sure!" Kasey exclaimed as she held out her arms. "Come here, my little man!"

Simeon's hands raced out to meet her as he squealed, "Kae-"

Sarah chuckled. "We've been trying, but he still hasn't got the hang of the '-sey'."

"Aren't you the cutest?" Kasey blurted, pulling him into a tight hug. "Boy you've certainly gotten heavier since I last saw you. Who's a big boy?"

Simeon wrapped his arms around Kasey, giggling madly as she squeezed him tighter. Hearing him laugh smashed the tension she had been struggling under for days.

Oh, I've needed this. Despite being home to eight and a half million people, New York could feel like a lonely place at times.

Sarah grabbed the door and Kasey followed her out onto the bustling New York City Street.

Kasey's stomach growled. "I could really go for a bagel and some coffee,"

"Then the cafe on St Mark's Place will be perfect," Sarah replied happily. "They do a mean bagel."

"Lead the way," Kasey answered, shifting Simeon to her hip so she could carry him more easily.

Sarah strolled down East 5th Street. "So, sis, what has you all worked up? Not often I get an S.O.S text from you these days. Come to think of it, I can only remember one of them, and that was way back in the Academy."

Kasey sighed. "I don't know where to begin."

"How about why you are at the NYPD instead of the OCME?" Sarah answered. "The OCME was your goal for years. I was shocked when I heard you'd transferred."

"Very well," Kasey said. "I really loved working at the OCME, but unfortunately one of my colleagues was a bit of a pig. He asked me out repeatedly, even after I'd said no and then one day when I was looking in the refrigerator...he spanked me."

"He spanked you?" Sarah asked, aghast.

"Yeah," Kasey answered, a little embarrassed.

Sarah stopped at the crosswalk and turned to face Kasey. "Did you report him?"

"I didn't get the chance."

"What do you mean, you didn't get the chance? That is clear cut sexual harassment, Kasey," Sarah replied, shaking her hand for emphasis.

"I snapped. I hit him and broke three of his ribs. There wasn't a lot of point to reporting him after that. The Chief Medical Examiner was gracious enough to get me a transfer rather than fire me outright, and the pig dropped the assault charges when it was clear his harassment was common knowledge. If I pushed any harder, I might have lost my license."

"I'm sorry to hear that, Kasey. That sucks."

The signal on the crosswalk changed to green and they stepped onto the street.

"I was pretty mad about it at first," Kasey began, "but over the last two weeks I've really enjoyed working at the Ninth Precinct."

"Really?" Sarah said, unconvinced.

"Yeah, I feel like my work here is making a difference. The work I do can solve a case and put a killer behind bars. It's not quite the bag and tag routine I was used to, but turns out I enjoy being a little closer to the front lines."

Sarah continued walking down First Avenue "So, if you're enjoying it here, what has you in such a panic, Kasey? It's not like you."

"It has to do with the case I'm working at the moment," Kasey answered, slowly working up the courage to spill the details. "We're hunting a serial killer operating in Manhattan. He's killed three people, that we know of, and that is just this week."

Sarah's face fell. "Three this week? How is that not in the news, Kasey? That's horrible."

"We only connected the dots last night and Chief West has been trying to avoid a panic. Besides, we got lucky. We found a list of his targets so there is no need to panic the rest of the city."

"What about the targets, Kasey? Surely they deserve to know," Sarah insisted.

"Of course, they do," Kasey said, "but that is where it gets a little complicated."

"How so?" Sarah replied, her tone reflecting her growing skepticism.

"Well, we rounded up the targets and we have them in police protection. The killer won't be able to reach them without going through an entire precinct. Not a healthy proposition."

"But Kasey, these sorts aren't often in their right mind. It's the crazy ones you have to watch out for. I'm not sure I like the sound of your new job."

"It gets worse," Kasey replied reluctantly.

"How is that even possible?"

"Oh, that's easy," Kasey said. "You know that list of targets I mentioned..."

"Yeah..."

"I'm on it," Kasey said flatly.

Sarah stopped mid stride as she whirled to face her. "What do you mean, you're on the list? Are you crazy? Why are we outside the station?"

"Easy, Sarah. We're not in danger. It's mid-morning in one of the busiest cities on Earth. We'll be fine."

"How can you know that? He's a nut job and a killer, Kasey. Who knows what he's capable of?"

"I'm getting to that part. You should know I'd never put you or Simeon at risk."

Sarah didn't look convinced.

Kasey nodded toward the street. "Mind if we keep walking? He's getting a little heavier than I expected."

"Sure," Sarah replied, still looking white with shock.

Kasey continued her story. "When I found out I was a target, I thought about camping out at the station, but Sarah, my visions are helping us find this guy."

"You're still seeing those?" Sarah asked. The gift of prescience wasn't hereditary. "I thought those stopped after you left the Academy."

"They certainly became rarer. It seems the presence of other witches and wizards strengthens my gift. The Academy was an overwhelming environment. I couldn't cope with such a concentrated number of magical beings. Here it is far easier for me. The visions are less frequent but often they help us solve a case. They helped us find the killer's lair and locate his list of targets. Without it, we'd still be scurrying around blindly."

Sarah shook her head. "How do you explain your gift to the police? You know how the Council feels about discovery. You need to be careful."

"I am!" Kasey said. As Sarah recoiled, Kasey flushed red. "Sorry, I'm a little on edge. I am careful not to give them too much. Mostly they figure I'm just good at my job. I just have to be careful not to be too good."

"That's a fine line, Kasey," Sarah replied as they turned down St Marks Place.

"You're telling me," Kasey said. "I'm still getting the hang of it."

"So, do you have any idea who the killer is?" Sarah asked. "Have you seen them in a vision?"

"No, I did one better. I saw him in the flesh. He's the one responsible for most of this," Kasey said as she pointed to her scrapes and cuts. "He tossed me through a window."

Sarah grabbed Kasey by the arm. "Have you lost your mind? What were you doing that close to a serial killer?"

"Well, truth be told, I wasn't expecting him to be there. We thought he'd fled town. I worked out where he'd been laying low and searched the place. It's how we found the list."

Sarah's eyes were wide. "What did he look like? Surely the precinct can send out an alert."

"That's where it gets complicated," Kasey said.

"How is that complicated? Did you see him or not?"

Kasey pulled away from Sarah's grip. "I did. The problem is, when I saw him, he was a giant hulking wolf." She paused as Sarah caught up. "The killer is one of us, Sarah. He's a creature of magic, definitely a shifter, a Werewolf."

Sarah did the math. "So, you don't know what he looks like in his human form and you can't go telling your colleagues that they are hunting a Werewolf. Doing so will surely anger the ADI and for what? It's not like they will believe your serial killer is a Werewolf. Let's face it, they are going to think you're crazy."

"Exactly. So, you see why I can't sit on the sidelines. If I do nothing, more innocent people will die. What chance does a police officer stand against a Werewolf? If that wasn't motivation enough, I have strict orders from the Council. I have to stop this killer, and I have to do it without outing our community, or else."

"How do they even know you exist, Kasey? I thought you never registered."

"I didn't. Unfortunately, I caught their attention by accident."

"How did you manage that?" Sarah asked, her tone dire.

"You know the pig I mentioned at the OCME?"

Sarah stopped walking. "Yeah, what about him?"

"Did I mention his name was John Ainsley, the son of Arthur Ainsley?"

Sarah's eyes went wide. She'd graduated from the Academy and grown up in the world of magic. Unlike Kasey, she clearly knew exactly who they were. "What?"

"Yeah, I had no idea who he was. Not like he was wearing a badge that said, 'Hi, I'm a wizard...and a sexist pig.' Turns out, it got their attention."

"You assaulted the son of a sitting Chancellor, Kasey. You've gone off the deep end." Sarah resumed her march up St Mark's Place.

"Hey, I said I didn't know!" Kasey replied chasing after her. "Between assaulting his son and using my magic without registering with the Council, he has me in a tough spot."

"He's blackmailing you?" Sarah answered in disgust.

Kasey replied, "Well, he didn't use those exact words, but it was certainly the theme of his visit. If I can make this killer go away quietly, they'll drop it and leave me alone. If our community is discovered, they plan to use me as a scapegoat."

"That's awful. I'm starting to see why you sent that text. I don't know how you are managing to hold things together this well. Do Mom and Dad know about this?"

"No," Kasey answered as they reached the cafe, "and they aren't going to."

"You're crazy, Kasey." Sarah opened the door and the aroma of freshly ground coffee beans wafted out to meet them. "If they find out..."

"They aren't going to find out, Sarah, because I'm not going to tell them, and you are the only other person who knows anything."

Kasey stepped inside. The morning rush was over and there were only a few other patrons waiting to be served.

She went straight for the counter, Sarah trailing behind her. Talking to the barista, Kasey began, "I'll grab two bagels with cream cheese and...one sec." She turned to Sarah. "What are you having?"

"I'll grab a cream cheese bagel and a cappuccino," Sarah said, coming up behind her and kissing the top of Simeon's head.

"Anything for our big boy?" Kasey asked.

Sarah shook her head. "No, thanks, I'll share a little of mine with him."

Turning back to the barista, Kasey continued, "Make that three cream cheese bagels and two cappuccinos, please."

Kasey paid for breakfast and stepped away from the counter just in time to prevent Simeon from pulling the tip jar off the counter.

Sarah approached her. "So, what is your plan exactly? Are you planning to use yourself as bait to catch this guy?"

"I dunno." Kasey shrugged. "Still working that part out. I've only met the one Werewolf so I'm still playing catch-up."

Sarah nodded. "You missed a lot when you left the Academy."

"Starting to feel that pretty keenly, sis," Kasey replied.

"I think we'll skip the park today. You need some help, or you are going to get yourself killed."

"I don't think we'll find many volunteers, Sarah."

"Not that sort of help, Kasey. You might do well in a ring but you're going to need more than your mixed martial arts to best a beast like that. You're going to need the right tool for the job...You're going to need The Emporium."

CHAPTER 14

Kasey cocked her head. "The Emporium?"

"Oh, yes," Sarah answered. "If you are going to run into the jaws of death, let us make sure you are suitably armed."

"I've never even heard of it," Kasey answered.

Sarah shook her head. "Come on, Kasey. You can't keep living with one foot in each world. If you are going to dabble in the arcane, you need to know what you are dealing with. The Emporium is the Convenience Co. of Magic. If a witch or wizard needs it, you'll find it at the Emporium..."

The barista's voice interrupted Sarah's explanation. "Two cappuccinos and three cream cheese bagels."

Sarah slipped over to the counter and picked up the coffee and bagels.

"Thanks!" she called to the barista who was already bustling away on the next order. She turned to Kasey to find Simeon trying to climb over her shoulder. "Here, let me swap you, breakfast for my baby."

Kasey eyed the bagel, her famished stomach groaning in protest. "Fine, but I'm going to want another cuddle when I'm done."

Sarah replied, "Absolutely, but first, we're going shopping!"

Kasey handed Simeon to his mother in exchange for the scrumptious-looking breakfast.

"Let's talk and walk. It'll take us a few minutes to get there," Sarah said as she made her way to the cafe's door.

Kasey nodded as she grabbed the handle and opened it. Holding it with her foot, she pulled her bagel out of its paper bag and took a bite. A muffled, "Mmm," escaped her lips.

"That hits the spot," she said as she grabbed the second bagel and handed it to her sister.

Sarah led Kasey through Tompkins Square Park and down East 9th Street, eating and gossiping as they went.

After a few minutes, Sarah reached out to stop Kasey. "Here we are."

Kasey looked up at an old brick apartment building with a shopfront built into its ground floor. A set of concrete stairs led into the store. Small white vinyl letters in the window read, 'Museum of Reclaimed Urban Space'.

Kasey raised her eyebrow as she fixed her sister with a dubious expression. "This is The Emporium? Certainly looks like it has seen better days."

"Looks can be deceiving, Kasey," Sarah replied. "In the 80's, these buildings were at the heart of a dispute between the city and squatters who had taken up residence here. After decades of disputes, Ernesto Thompson, in conjunction with the Mayor's office, granted ownership of the buildings to the Urban Homesteading and Assistance Board. In exchange for his aid in ending the conflict, Ernesto was allowed to purchase the building, C-Squat. He now runs tours promoting the cultural history of the area."

"I'm not sure what that has to do with The Emporium," Kasey replied.

"Well, after getting rid of a few punk rockers and a half pipe in the basement, C-Squat gave him the perfect home for his growing enterprise—the purveying of magical goods. He erected the museum as a tribute to both the cultural heritage and his sense of humor."

"Sense of humor?"

"Oh, you'll see soon enough," Sarah said, ascending the stone stairs.

A woman in uniform greeted them as they entered the Museum, "Hello, and welcome to the Museum of Reclaimed Urban Space, or MORUS for short. Are you here for the tour?"

"Not today, dear. We'll be needing the gift shop," Sarah said.

The woman nodded. "Very well, would you like me to show you the way?"

"That won't be necessary. I've known Ernesto for years," Sarah replied heading deeper into the store.

The woman smiled. "Very well. Have a wonderful day."

"Thanks," Sarah replied as she dragged Kasey through the small museum. Rounding a corner, they entered a narrow corridor. On the left stood a set of restrooms. On the right, a small closet marked, 'Cleaning'.

"Ah, here we are!" Sarah exclaimed as she reached out and grabbed the handle of the cleaning closet.

"A closet?" Kasey asked. Sarah had to be messing with her.

Sarah pulled open the door and gestured onward. "Precisely. Now in you go."

Kasey shrugged and stepped into the cramped space. Her foot bumped something on the floor. Reaching down, she picked up a fallen mop and leaned it against the wall to make more room. She turned to face Sarah.

Sarah squeezed in next to her, pulling the closet door shut. Darkness concealed them.

"Disgyn," Sarah chanted.

Kasey wracked her brain for the meaning of the Welsh phrase.

The entire room shuddered. Kasey gripped the shelves to stay on her feet but began to experience the same weightless sensation she loathed on roller-coasters.

It's an elevator.

The entire closet was descending at incredible speed. Her full stomach felt a little queasy.

"Sarah, you... could... have... warned... me," she said between breaths.

"Don't fret, we're almost there," Sarah said.

As if on cue, the elevator slowed its descent. A purple orb of light flickered to life where the closet door had been, pale at first but increasing in intensity.

Without warning, it began to flit about, leaving a shimmering trail of purple behind it in the air. Kasey watched spellbound as the light moved as if borne by an invisible hand. With precision, it worked until the word 'Welcome' shimmered in the air before them.

The closet door swung open. Kasey's jaw dropped. Rich timber walls met elegant marble floors in a display of cleanly-styled affluence. Opposite the elevator, a large information counter occupied most of the store front, filling the space on either side were a dozen checkouts manned by cashiers. Each wore a pinstripe suit or pantsuit that reminded Kasey of the mob era movies of the 1920s and 30s.

Sarah made straight for the counter. It bore an immense engraved placard bearing the store's name in bold script.

"Sarah, how nice to see you again," a voice boomed across the lobby. The voice belonged to a sharply dressed man in an Italian suit standing behind the counter.

Sarah beamed. "Ernesto, how are you?"

Ernesto walked around the counter as he replied, "I am exceptional, thank you for asking. Is that Simeon? How he has grown! Tell me, did he enjoy his little birthday present?"

"Loves it to death," Sarah answered. "He chases that little pixie around the nursery for hours. He named her Bella."

Ernesto beamed. "Ah, Bella, I love it. Portland Pixies, capricious little creatures but full of energy. Perfect for tiring the little ones out before bed."

Portland Pixies? Kasey had never heard of such creatures.

"Indeed, it's worked like a charm," Sarah continued. "Paul, on the other hand, not as big a fan. Bella has a habit of hiding his keys. She thinks it's a game, but enough about me. How are Elvira and William?"

"Elvira is ecstatic. William is engaged to a charming young witch from Surrey. His mother will be thrilled to have him out of the house."

"Congratulations!" Sarah exclaimed, throwing one arm around him while she clutched Simeon with the other. "When is the big day?"

Ernesto replied embracing Sarah, "Thank you. It's not set in stone yet, but we expect it will be in the summer."

"How charming," Sarah replied as she stepped back. She gestured at Kasey. "Ah, forgive me, Ernesto. This is my sister Kasey. Kasey, Ernesto. Ernesto's son William and I were in the Academy together."

"I should have known!" Ernesto exclaimed, embracing Kasey. "The resemblance is unmistakable. A Stonemoore if ever I've seen one."

Kasey returned the embrace. "Ernesto, a pleasure."

He glanced from sister to sister. "So, what brings you both to The Emporium? How can I be of service?"

"Ernesto, no need to trouble yourself. We're just looking for a few supplies. Kasey has a little bit of a pest problem," Sarah explained.

"It's no trouble at all. Mornings are usually our quiet time anyway."

Kasey's eyes wandered while Sarah spoke. Old timber shelves formed aisles stretching as far as the eye could see. The Emporium must have covered more than a city block. Dozens of patrons bustled through the store. Kasey didn't even know where to begin.

Ernesto placed an arm around each sister and steered them into the store. "Now, what is it you are looking for? A pest problem you said. I take it is of the magical variety?"

"Sure is, Ernesto," Sarah said. "Some Pest-Kill Plus just isn't going to cut it."

Ernesto rubbed his chin. "So, what are we dealing with? A sly little leprechaun? Maybe some Chameleonic Garden Gnomes? Whatever it is, we'll have just the thing."

He set out down the aisles.

Kasey had to take a few quick steps to keep up. "Ernesto, I don't know what a Chameleonic Garden Gnome is, but we need something that will kill a Werewolf."

Ernesto stopped dead. He turned slowly to face her. "Miss Stonemoore, a Werewolf is not a pest. They are accepted members of the magical community. They have rights, have had for almost 400 years. The killing of a Werewolf is criminal conduct. It is punishable by the Council. I'd advise you to reconsider."

Kasey stepped closer to Ernesto to not be overheard. "Look, Ernesto, I don't want to kill anyone, but this Werewolf is stalking me. He has already killed two other young women and there is every chance that I'm next." Kasey pointed to her wounds from Hudson Road. The bruises had faded somewhat but the cuts were still fresh. "He threw me through a window. I need something that can stop him before he finishes the job."

It sounded like begging, and Kasey hated it. Unfortunately, the last few days had drained her, both physically and emotionally. "Ernesto, please, it's a matter of life and death."

Ernesto examined her, his expression unreadable. "Very well, Miss Stonemoore. I don't condone the use of violence, but one must be able to protect themselves. What you need, however, cannot be found among our normal magical supplies. We'll need to go to the Beastiary."

"The Beastiary?" Kasey glanced at Sarah. "Where and what is that?"

Ernesto leaned closer. "The Beastiary is where we keep our more exotic items, those that would not be smiled upon by our more discerning clientele."

"Sounds like what I'm after," Kasey replied, she was anxious for any advantage over the beast.

"Very well. The Beastiary is no place for children. Sarah, you will need to leave Simeon in the creche with the other youngsters. It's for his own safety," Ernesto said as he waved over one of his clerks.

Sarah hugged Simeon tight before handing him to the clerk. "Have fun. Momma will be back soon."

"Follow me," Ernesto said. He turned on his heel and led them deeper into the Emporium.

Kasey stared in wonder as she passed row upon row of shelves labeled with goods she had never even imagined: Potions and Powders, Arcane Artifacts, Bathista's Bites and Meals for Mythical Beasts, Self-Reading Papers, Destiny and Divination.

She supposed she could spend hours exploring the marvels of The Emporium and her curious nature wanted to do just that. She regretted neglecting her heritage. It had been easy to turn a blind eye to magic after leaving the Academy. It wasn't until she was striding down the aisles of the sprawling store that she began to come to grips with just how ignorant she was of her own people.

There will be a time and a place to fix that, but right now, I need to stay alive.

Ernesto led them into an aisle filled with mirrors. Kasey made her way down it, glancing in the glass as she went. Each had a different effect on her reflection. Some made her appear thinner, others taller or shorter. One in particular made her pause: an ornate full-length mirror in a polished bronze frame. The frame itself had elegant silver and gold inlay in a Celtic pattern. It was beautiful. A sold sign rested at its base.

Kasey stared into the glass but no reflection greeted her. She could see Sarah and Ernesto but not herself. It was more than a little disconcerting.

"Come here, Kasey," Ernesto called from farther down the aisle.

Kasey glanced back at the mirror, then hurried to catch up with the others.

Ernesto was standing in front of a large full-length mirror with a beautiful polished silver frame. It had no label or price tag.

He reached out and placed his palm on the mirror. Closing his eyes, he chanted, "Revelare!"

The surface of the mirror swirled before disappearing entirely. Instead, a stone chamber became visible, as if the mirror had somehow become a window.

"Come now, we must hurry." Ernesto tested the portal with his hand. Its surface rippled as his arm passed through. Satisfied that all was in order, Ernesto plunged through the fluid surface, small waves rolled outward until they struck the edge of the frame.

Not wishing to be left behind, Kasey approached the shimmering surface. Following Ernesto's lead, she tested the portal. As her hand returned safely, she mustered the courage and leaped through the portal.

Kasey felt like she had been submerged underwater, then in an instant the feeling passed and she found herself standing in the stone chamber with Ernesto.

Reflexively, she gasped for air.

Seconds later, Sarah emerged behind them.

Ernesto swept his hand across the surface of a matching mirror.

"Celare," he said, his heavy English accent reverberating around the chamber.

The portal vanished. Bricks re-materializing where it had just been.

"Where are we, Ernesto?" Kasey asked.

The cold gray stone walls were markedly different to the elegant Emporium they had been standing in only moments earlier. Where had the portal had taken her?

"Welcome to the Beastiary," Ernesto said. "It is where I store items that are not fit for general consumption or use. It wouldn't do to have a child stumbling upon a cursed artifact, now would it?"

"Why would you even keep a cursed artifact?" Kasey asked. The whole notion was backwards.

"Because, Miss Stonemoore, each customer has a different need. What one sees as a curse, another might see as a blessing. Shoes of ceaseless wandering might be torture for one patron, but for someone who has been lame their whole life, might provide them the giddy joy of a sensation they had never expected to experience.

"My business is to meet my patron's needs and wishes. Understanding and identifying the inherent value of an item is fundamental to my family's success. The item you seek, for instance, Werewolves would shun, but to you it will be the instrument of your salvation."

Kasey surveyed the chamber. The shelves in the dimly lit room were of a sturdy steel construction. They were covered in a bizarre assortment of objects: a pair of dirty running shoes, a glass egg-timer, an empty snow-globe. There was even an entire plastic skeleton resting on a shelf in the center of the room.

"Ernesto, what is the skeleton for? It's obviously not real. What purpose does it serve?"

His mouth peaked into a smile. "That is my security system, Miss Stonemoore. Should anyone attempt to gain access to the vault without me, an alarm will trigger and Bagabones will ensure they do not steal anything."

Kasey studied the crumpled skeleton resting on the shelf. It looked like it had been kicked down a flight of stairs.

That's about as dangerous as a wet paper bag.

Her doubt must have been evident, as Ernesto continued. "I assure you, he is quite capable, Miss Stonemoore. In all my years as the owner of this establishment, I have never lost an item from this vault. Do you wish to see him in action?"

Kasey was intrigued. "Sure, bring it on."

"Very well," Ernesto answered. "If you wouldn't mind taking a few steps forward, I'll trigger the alarm."

Kasey took three steps toward the skeleton. Without conscious thought, she took up a ready stance.

"Terrorem!" Ernesto said from behind her.

Two blue orbs appeared in the skull's eye sockets, the skeletal jaw extended and retracted as if the creature was stretching. There was a clattering noise as the skeleton unfurled itself. It rested its weathered arms on the shelf and propelled itself clear. The skeleton landed deftly on the stone chamber floor and lumbered toward Kasey.

Bagabones took two more steps before dropping into a lunge and launching itself at her.

As the skeleton sailed toward her, she nimbly side stepped the enchanted skeleton. Bagabones snarled. She dipped left and delivered a punishing roundhouse kick to the creature as it sailed past her. The kick struck Bagabones in the hip, sweeping his legs out from under him.

He came down hard, landing on his side and skidding into the wall. His skull struck with enough force that it would have knocked out a boxer. Sarah gave a victory whoop, and Kasey broke into a satisfied grin.

Her smile faded as the skeleton shook its head as if it were waking up. Slowly, it raised itself off the ground and got back to its feet.

"Got a little fight in you huh?" Kasey asked as it approached.

"Miss Stonemoore," Ernesto said from where he leaned against a shelf. "Rest assured he's not delicate, despite his appearance. No need to be gentle."

His reassurance sounded like a taunt. Time to up the ante.

She waited for the creature to close once more. As it neared, it flexed its hand. Then it swung its fist at her. Kasey dodged left once more. Bagabones launched a vicious right-handed hook.

Kasey ducked under the blow and grabbed the creature's left wrist. Using Bagabones' momentum against him, she turned and, dropping her shoulder into his bony torso, brutally flipping the creature.

Bagabones thundered headfirst into the stone floor.

Kasey, still holding the creature's arm, twisted it violently. The movement would have left a human opponent in agony.

Bagabones arm snapped clean off at the shoulder. It was a bizarre scene as Kasey held the disembodied skeletal arm while the creature struggled to its feet once more. This time, the creature was slower as he struggled to compensate for his missing limb.

Kasey looked at Ernesto who just stared back impassively.

No more playing. It is time to end this.

She sized up the skeleton before her. She had no reference for fighting magical creatures, but the skeletal guard must have a breaking point.

As Bagabones rose from the floor, Kasey flipped the skeletal arm so that she was holding it by the bicep. Gripping the bone with both hands, she swung it with all her might.

CHAPTER 15

There was a deafening crack as bone struck bone.

The skeletal guard exploded in spectacular fashion. The skull with its glowing eyes burst free from its neck like a baseball soaring for the grandstands.

It struck the rear wall with a gratifying crack. The headless skeleton tottered for a moment before crashing to the ground in a noisy heap.

The skeletal arm in Kasey's hands snapped at the elbow.

She tossed it aside, then turned to face Ernesto, dusting her hands as a satisfied smile spread across her face. "It's outta here!"

Ernesto simply pointed at the rear wall.

Kasey spun to see Bagabones' skull, lying on its side on the cobblestone floor staring back at her.

The blue orbs that served as eyes faded and went out.

Kasey let out a grunt of satisfaction.

Then the empty sockets blazed red and the skull began to shake.

"Oh..." Kasey cut herself off as the skull skittered across the floor toward her.

She leaped backward as the skeleton's bones gathered together. She watched with dread as the conjuration reassembled itself, reattaching its arm and hand as it stood up. Reaching down, Bagabones picked up his skull and reattached it. Staring Kasey down, he went to take a step but stopped. He grabbed hold of one of his skeletal ribs. With a sickening snap he broke the rib free and, brandishing it like a knife, charged at her.

Kasey's heart pounded as the creature closed, its grisly weapon raised for the kill.

"Prohibere!" Ernesto's voice rang out.

Bagabones stopped dead, turned on the spot, and marched back to his shelf. Upon reaching the shelf, he collapsed in a heap, the flaming eyes fading to empty sockets once more.

"Well, I think that is quite enough of that," Ernesto exclaimed.

Kasey shook her head. "What on Earth was that?"

"A skeletal sentinel," Ernesto replied. "Perhaps not the smartest of conjurations, but you just can't beat them for durability."

"How do you stop something like that?" she demanded.

"You don't," Ernesto answered calmly, "but then again, I believe that's the point. That particular sentinel has been in our family for three centuries and he's still going strong."

"I've never seen anything like it," Kasey admitted.

"Most people have not," Ernesto answered as he straightened his suit. "They are extremely rare. Originally crafted by a family of Persian artisans around 500BC. Unfortunately, the family were put to death by Cyrus the Great for Necromancy. Fortunately for us, the sentinels were far more durable than their masters and several of them still survive to the present day."

"Fortunately?" Sarah shook her head. "That thing was terrifying. We could do with a few less of those in the world in my opinion."

"Oh, the sentinel is nothing to worry about. He's only a threat to those who break into the vault. You've come as welcome guests, so fear not! Now let us see what we have to help you with your Werewolf issue."

Ernesto moved along the shelves and began searching for something. "I know it is here somewhere."

He rifled through the shelves; his pace increasingly frantic.

"Do you need a hand?" Sarah asked following Ernesto along the shelf.

"No, thank you, Sarah," Ernesto replied holding up his hand, "I'm sorry. I never lose anything. I simply need to remember precisely where I left it."

Kasey and Sarah looked at each other and smiled. Together they waited as he made his way through the chamber, simultaneously sifting through and sorting the relics as he went.

"Aha!" he exclaimed, lifting a small box into the air. "I knew it was here somewhere."

He made his way back to Kasey and Sarah, clutching the small box protectively in both hands. The ornate case was carved from a dark timber. On its surface it had three intricately formed interlocking triangles.

"What do you know about Werewolves, Miss Stonemoore?" Ernesto asked.

"Only what I've seen firsthand. Hulking great beasts that are lightning quick, not to mention the mouthful of teeth that could tear me to shreds. Oh, and they can take a punch. Kind of why we are here, Ernesto. Not sure what I can do to stop one should the need arise."

Ernesto nodded. "I see. Well, they certainly are impressive, but they aren't immortal. They can take a beating and they may seem infallible. Fortunately, experience has taught us that they do indeed have a weakness. Silver."

"Silver?" Sarah asked. "I thought that was an old wives' tale."

"Based in reality, I assure you," Ernesto replied. "The quickest way to slay a Werewolf is to strike it in the heart with pure silver. The beast's heart will stop beating immediately. In the 1800s, the Europeans dealt with their Werewolf scourge by fashioning silver balls for their muskets and pistols.

"When the Treaty of Thames extended sanctuary to Werewolves as accepted members of the magical community, the manufacturing of weapons designed to kill them all but dried up. Fortunately, this artifact has its origins in a time far before that, when men didn't have the luxury of a gun to put distance between him and his lupine foe."

Ernesto opened the small box and produced a glimmering shard of silver. It was almost the size of a pen. The shard fit neatly in his fist as he held it aloft.

"What precisely am I meant to do with that, Ernesto?" Kasey asked, distinctly underwhelmed. "Hope he eats it by mistake?"

Ernesto's face fell. "My mistake. I keep forgetting, history is a subject often eschewed in the schools of today." Tapping the top of the box, he said, "This is the Valknut, ancient and sacred symbol of the Norse. It is the mark of the god Odin. If you want a lesson in dealing with Werewolves, you best take it from those who triumphed over them in the first place.

"Scandinavia was where the lupine disease first appeared and spread. The Norse were a fiercely proud people. Unwilling to abandon their homes, they banded together and drove the beasts out of their lands. Unfortunately, their victory was Europe's condemnation, as the dreaded curse spread like wildfire among the Vikings' less hardy neighbors."

"That's fascinating, Ernesto, but I still don't see how a silver pen is going to make much of a dint. He'll tear me apart before I can get close enough to shank him with that," Kasey replied.

"Patience, Miss Stonemoore, I will not entrust you with a relic of such historic import unless you understand both its cultural significance and its priceless nature."

Kasey conceded the point. "My apologies, Ernesto. Please continue."

"This is no mere shard of silver. It is the very blade by which the Norse drove the beasts from their lands." He spun the shard with a flourish, "It is Gungnir!"

Kasey and Sarah stared dumbfounded at Ernesto.

"Are you kidding me?" Ernesto answered, exasperated. "You have no idea what Gungnir is, do you? What do they even teach in school these days?"

Kasey shook her head. "Sorry, I took Math and English. Never mentioned a Gungnir that I can remember."

Ernesto looked like he might burst a vein. "Math and English...what? Did you not attend the Academy?"

Kasey sighed. "Yes and no. I was there but not for long. I finished my schooling here in New York."

Ernesto nodded slowly. "Well, that explains a lot. A little odd for a Stonemoore but... as they say, it's a new world."

"I went to the Academy, Ernesto, but I didn't hear anything about Gungnir, either," Sarah chimed in.

"Well, then, let me make up for that educational oversight," he answered. "Perhaps it's because most believe Gungnir to be a myth, fabricated by the Norsemen to scare their enemies. The Werewolves of Scandinavia on the other hand, know it to be real. They felt its deadly bite as it scattered them before it." He raised the silver shard above his head and cried out, "Afpvi at Odin!"

The alien phrase echoed around the small chamber. Ernesto's previous incantations has been in Old Latin. That much had been clear to Kasey from her time in the Academy. This was something else entirely. It differed from the Welsh she used in her own spells.

As Kasey puzzled over the meaning of the words Ernesto had used, Gungnir shimmered, the shard of silver expanding rapidly, issuing a distinct ring. The sound mimicked the noise of a sword clearing its scabbard. The shard elongated to a wicked point. When it reached six feet, it stopped growing and a series of intricate raised lines appeared in its surface.

"It's a spear!" Kasey declared.

"No, Kasey," Ernesto whispered. "Not a spear—the spear. The Spear of Odin!"

"Odin? Thor's dad? The god from all those superhero movies?" Kasey asked, taking in the impressive weapon. "I thought they were fiction."

Ernesto laughed. "They are. I assure you. But like most of Hollywood's better film forays, there is a kernel of truth at its core. Odin wasn't a god, though he might as well have been.

"He was a Norse wizard who forged weapons of power for the north men. One day, he was working in his forge when a pack of Werewolves attacked his farm. He took up arms to defend his family, but they were all slain.

"Odin himself was trapped, his back to a wall. In one hand he held his smith's hammer, in the other a sword he had been forging for the King. It was not meant for battle; it was a gift to honor the success of his raids. The blade was forged from solid silver—silver stolen from my own homeland, England.

"As the beasts advanced, Odin fought like a man possessed. The hammer may have annoyed the beasts, but the silver sword sowed death with every stroke.

"When the villagers found him, Odin alone was still standing, surrounded on all sides by slain Werewolves. When his rage subsided, he realized he held in his hands the secret to stopping the beasts that plagued his homeland.

"So, he melted down the sword and forged a spear. It was the finest weapon he had ever crafted. Concealing it with a shrinking spell, Odin hid its true nature so no other than him could wield it. Fueled by a desire for revenge for his family's death, Odin went after the beasts. With each success, his fame grew. Vikings flocked to his banner. Soon, Odin the Smith was forgotten, and Odin the Warrior-God was born. He pursued the Werewolves from ocean to ocean, driving them from the north.

"To the Vikings, he was a God among men, but like all men he eventually passed from this world. The secret of his craft and his legendary spear were lost for centuries, until my family found it. We could sense the magic that lay within, but it took us decades to unlock its mysteries. Now you can see it in all its glory.

"When it comes to Werewolves, there is no finer weapon. To them, it is as deadly as it is terrifying. It may have been lost for centuries, but you better believe they have not forgotten it. The once indomitable beasts have been on the run ever since... at least until the Treaty of Thames."

"Sounds like just the thing I need," Kasey said, reaching for the spear.

Ernesto lowered the spear but did not hand it over. "Miss Stonemoore, the Spear of Odin is a priceless artifact, one that has been in our family for hundreds of years. I could never sell it..."

Kasey's face fell, the hopes that had been building inside her dashed.

Ernesto continued, "But I could lend it to you for safekeeping... at least until we find you something else. There is, however, a favor I would ask of you, after all The Emporium is not simply a library service for lethal weapons."

"Of course," Kasey answered, relieved that she wouldn't be leaving empty handed, "What can I do Ernesto?"

Ernesto's face remained impassive. "As I mentioned, the spear is a priceless heirloom, but there is something I have been after for many years. It just so happens that your father has in his possession a small jewelry box. I have been trying to purchase it from him for decades, but he is most determined. If you could put in a good word for me, I would be most grateful."

Kasey was disappointed. "Ernesto, I need that spear, and I will certainly put in a good word for you, but I can't give any assurances that he will part with it."

Ernesto raised his hand. "I don't need an assurance, Miss Stonemoore, just your word that you will relate to him the part my family and I have played in aiding you. My family has been in this business for generations, and we know that a little goodwill goes a long way. So, what do you say, Kasey? Can I count on you?"

"Of course," Kasey replied. "That much I can do."

"Very well, then. It is yours, Kasey, at least for a season. Ensure you bring it back to me safely." He held out the spear.

Kasey took the offered spear. As soon as Ernesto release the weapon, it shrunk back to its former size.

"Wow!" Kasey exclaimed, "I guess I wasn't quite ready for that."

Ernesto laughed. "I hope you weren't expecting to walk the streets of New York carrying a spear. Don't worry, you can activate its power anytime you wish. All you must do is summon its power as I did. Do you remember the incantation?"

Kasey nodded as she raised the shard. "Afpvi at Odin!"

CHAPTER 16

Kasey bid a hasty goodbye to Sarah and Simeon and raced back to the Ninth Precinct.

"You have one new voice message," Kasey's cell phone declared. Kasey fingers raced across her phone as she dialed her voice mail.

"Kasey where the hell have you gone?" Bishop's recorded voice shouted from her phone. "I've been trying you for hours. Just pick up your stinking phone. If it wasn't clear last night, you're not meant to leave the station without an escort." Bishop's voice paused. "It's not safe, Kasey. Call me back. I'm worried about you."

Oh, crap. Kasey flicked through her phone. Seventeen missed calls.

Oh, boy, I'm in trouble.

She hadn't realized just how much time had passed while she was with Sarah.

In her heart, Kasey knew she should have asked Bishop before leaving. But she also knew what Bishop's answer would be, and Kasey couldn't bear to be cooped up in the station any longer.

Besides, she wasn't going to find the killer by hiding and Arthur Ainsley had made it abundantly clear that failure was not an option. She had considered using herself as bait but that hadn't been a particularly appealing scenario. Not before, anyway.

Armed and dangerous, Kasey reconsidered her options as she fidgeted with the silver shard resting in her pocket. The Spear of Odin was an impressive weapon. She hoped it would be enough to level the playing field.

Now she just had to find a way to draw the beast out of hiding without being observed by any non-magical beings.

Kasey yanked open the door to the station and made a beeline for the morgue. She was barely across the foyer before Bishop caught up with her.

"Kasey, where have you been? I have been worried sick. We thought the killer had you"

Kasey rubbed her stomach as she walked. "Sorry, Bishop, I was famished. I stepped out to get a bite to eat with my sister. I didn't mean to worry you."

"Breakfast?" Bishop asked incredulously. "You risked your life to get some coffee?"

"Well, not just a coffee," Kasey answered. "I had some bagels too."

Bishop looked as though she might explode.

"Are you okay, Bishop? You're looking a little..."

"No, I'm not alright, Kasey! We have a serial killer terrorizing the city, three bodies in the morgue, and almost twenty others in protective custody across the city. If that wasn't bad enough, now we have the FBI looking over our shoulders and watching our every move.

"That being said, can you imagine how it looks when my partner, a possible victim, goes AWOL in the middle of the investigation? Doesn't particularly send a message that inspires confidence."

Kasey stopped dead. "Wait, the FBI?"

"Yeah, one of their case officers showed up this morning. Word has gotten out about our little case and the mayor wants it wrapped up as soon as humanly possible.

"Now we have to do it while being scrutinized by the mayor, the media, and the FBI. As if doing our job wasn't hard enough already." Bishop swept a stray hair out of her face as she spoke.

Kasey could see that Bishop was having a rough time and her vanishing act clearly hadn't helped the cause. "I'm sorry, Bishop, I didn't mean to worry you, or make you look bad. It's been an awful week and I just needed something to eat. I thought I'd kill two birds with one stone and see my sister while I was at it. I won't do it again."

"Damn right you won't," Bishop answered, shaking her finger at Kasey. "You're not to leave the station without an escort."

"Understood," Kasey answered and held both hands up in a sign of surrender. She had nothing to argue. "Any new leads on the case?"

"Not yet. We've been busy dealing with the logistics of trying to guard all the potential victims. Our resources are being stretched to the limit. Between protecting these women and our usual workload, we are pretty thin on the ground right now.

"We've transferred a number of the victims to other precincts to try to spread the workload but it's a slow process. Not a lot of enthusiasm for babysitting duty. Vida is downstairs working on the victims' profiles. We are still trying to work out what the link between them is," Bishop answered.

"What, apart from the fact they all look like me?" Kasey used her fingers to frame her face.

"Yeah, I keep raising that with Vida," Bishop answered, "but he keeps insisting there is more to it than that. Keeps muttering that if that was the only criteria there would be far more women on the list. The victims while a broad spectrum, appear to have been painstakingly chosen. We just don't know why yet."

"We need to speak to the other girls," Kasey suggested. "The more information we have, the sooner we can piece all of this together."

"The FBI have been helping on that front. Agent Collins and I have been questioning them all morning."

"Agent Collins, huh? A little formal isn't it?"

"Formal is an understatement. I have seen more talkative suspects than this guy."

"Oh, sounds like a match made in heaven," Kasey teased. "Strong silent type. Just like you."

Bishop fixed her with a stare. "If you don't knock it off, I'm going to stick you in a cell. For your protection, of course."

Kasey laughed. "Where is he now?"

"He is across town interviewing one of our potential victims. She has a police detail from the Eighth Precinct.

"Collins wanted to finish his interviews today so he's on his way to her apartment to conduct it now. Sooner or later, we'll find the common thread that links them all, and the sooner the better..."

A cell phone ringing cut Bishop off. She looked annoyed until she found the ringing was coming from her own belt.

Bishop pulled out her phone, glanced at the number and waved for Kasey to follow her into a nearby office. Shutting the door behind them, Bishop answered the call by putting it on speaker. "What's up, Collins?"

There was no response, but in the background a door slammed, followed by a series of what sounded like gunshots.

Bishop frowned at the phone. "Collins, what the hell is going on?"

There was a string of labored breaths, followed by more gunshots.

"Collins?" Bishop was almost shouting.

"Bishop, it's me." The voice was deep but panicky. "We're under fire. I need backup."

"On our way, Collins! Where are you?"

"We're at the woman's apartment in Williamsburg, corner of Berry and 4th Street. We were helping her grab some clothes but the killer was already here..."

Another series of gunshots drowned out Collin's voice.

"Hurry, Bishop. I'm pinned down, and I've been cut off from the others. We need help."

"We're on our way, hang tight."

"Careful, Bishop, he's heavily armed. Bring the troops!"

"Roger that, Collins, we're on our way."

Bishop hung up the call and opened the office door.

She called the officer manning the station's front counter. "Georgiano, we have officers under fire and an active shooter," she shouted. "Corner of Berry and 4th Street Williamsburg. He's heavily armed. We'll need Tac. Support, and the paramedics. Make sure we have them ASAP."

"You got it, detective." Georgiano replied.

"Kasey let's go!" Bishop shouted, breaking into a run.

Kasey followed her across the building and out the double doors.

Reaching the parking lot, Bishop popped the trunk of her car and pulled out a bulletproof vest. She shoved one at Kasey. "Put this on."

Bishop opened a duffle bag in the trunk and pulled out a Glock 19. She checked the weapon, loaded a magazine, and handed it to Kasey.

"Whoa," Kasey answered.

"You've used a gun before, right?" Bishop asked.

"Yeah, the department tested me before they would let me go into the field."

"Excellent. It has a safety trigger, won't fire unless you put decent rearward pressure on it. Just follow my lead and you'll be fine."

Bishop grabbed a second vest from the trunk and swapped it for her jacket. Slamming the trunk, she nodded toward Kasey and then sprinted around to jump into the car. Kasey scrambled to keep up.

In seconds, Bishop had the car in gear and was tearing out of the parking lot.

Bishop covered the trip to Williamsburg in record time, sirens blared as she ducked and weaved her way through the busy streets. Reaching the corner of Berry and East 4th Streets, Kasey spotted the squad car out front and Bishop pulled in behind it.

Bishop jumped out of the car and drew her weapon. Kasey followed, keeping one hand resting on the shard of Odin's spear in her jeans pocket.

The street was deserted. Anyone who had heard the shots would have run a mile. Strangely, there was no sound coming from the building itself. Only minutes earlier, there had been dozens of shots echoing down the phone line. It didn't feel right.

Bishop clearly felt the same. "It's too quiet, Kasey. We can't wait."

"Are you sure that's wise, Bishop? Support shouldn't be far away."

"We can't afford to wait, Kasey. They could be injured or worse."

Kasey wasn't sure what to do, but Bishop made the choice for her. Gun in hand, she entered the building. Skipping the elevators, Bishop made for the stairs and Kasey followed.

"It's only the second floor. The elevator will take too long," Bishop explained.

Kasey nodded and followed her through the door and onto the stairs. She didn't relish the thought of coming face to face with the killer in such a confined space. With a gun, it would be like shooting fish in a barrel.

Bishop took the stairs two at a time.

Reaching the second floor, Bishop stepped out into the hallway. "There's an open door down there, Kasey. That must be it."

Kasey came up behind her and peered into the distance. There were no signs of a struggle. She stalked Bishop down the corridor, moving swiftly but quietly, searching for any sign of the shooter.

Reaching the open door, Bishop paused. Turning to Kasey she held up three fingers and quickly counted down to signal her intent. The gun felt strange in her hand, but it gave her some comfort.

Her magic was a potent tool for both offense and defense, but she couldn't summon her power in front of Bishop, so she was stuck relying on the weapon.

Her thoughts turned to the beast from Hudson Road and her pulse raced. She had known this moment was coming but still didn't feel ready for it.

Bishop reached the open door and swept into the room. Kasey held her breath as she rounded the corner.

They were too late. There were three bodies lying on the floor: Kelly Sachs, the killer's target, flanked by her police escort. They had been taken by surprise; neither of the officers had managed to draw a weapon. All three of them had been hit multiple times. While Bishop searched the room, Kasey hurried over to the bodies, and checked their vitals. No pulse. She turned to Bishop and shook her head, then scanned the room. There was no sign of the FBI agent, Collins.

"Collins!" Bishop called, as she made her way toward the bedroom.

"I'm in here," came the muffled response.

Kasey pointed to the bathroom. "It's coming from in there."

With Bishop in the lead, they made their way over to the bathroom door. There were three bullet holes, pock-marked across it. Bishop tried to peek through them before testing the lock. It was open. With her left hand on the handle and her right holding her gun, she eased open the door.

"Agent Collins!" Bishop exclaimed

Lying in the tub was a man. In his white shirt and tie he looked out of place.

"Easy, Bishop," the man called out with his hands up. "Pretty sure the killer's already gone. Once I started firing back, he lost interest fast."

Kasey followed Bishop over to the tub. A pool of red became visible in the base of the bath.

"You're hit!" Bishop exclaimed.

Collins had his hand pressed against his side, his fingers and the lower portion of his shirt stained red. "Yeah, he winged me as I came through the door. He mustn't have been expecting me. I got a few shots off and managed to make it in here.

"He shot up the door, but I was in the tub so I'm fine. I put another one through the door and he thought better of coming through it. The place has been quiet for a few minutes. I figured I'd wait for some backup before moving just in case."

"You don't need backup, you need a hospital," Kasey began, handing her gun to Bishop.

"Aw, it's not that bad," Collins replied. "I've certainly had worse. Pretty sure this one went straight through."

Kasey slid past Bishop, knelt and examined the wound in Collin's side. "Sure did, genius. So that hand of yours isn't doing a whole lot. We need to get you out of the tub and stitched up before you bleed out."

"No rest for the weary, huh?" Collins replied, trying to force a smile. "Who are you, anyway?"

"My apologies," Bishop interjected. "Agent Collins, meet Kasey Chase. She's our medical examiner and for the time being my crime scene tech as well. She's been assisting me with the case and if she says you need a hospital, Collins, that's where you are going."

Kasey chimed in, "I'm telling you, Collins, you've lost a lot of blood. If we don't get you stitched up, I'll be giving you a second opinion...when you're lying on the table in the morgue. Now stop being stubborn and let us help you out of that tub."

Collins was determined to get out on his own but his arm failed him and he fell backward against the tub. "Ow," was all he could manage through his gritted teeth.

Relenting, he reached out with his good hand. Kasey took his hand and Bishop hooked under his arm, and they heaved him to his feet.

"What happened to the others?" Collins asked. "Are they…"

"Dead," Bishop finished. "All of them. What the hell happened here?"

"The officers were escorting the woman here to pick up some medication and supplies. We had barely got inside the apartment when the shooting started. Big fella in a trench coat and ski mask came bursting out of the bedroom. Had some sort of machine pistol, hosed us down good. I managed to get off a couple of shots as I dived behind the couch. When he ducked into the kitchen, I made my way in here and shut the door. I'm sorry I couldn't reach the others. They were too exposed."

"Trying would have only got you killed, Collins. Let's get you downstairs. The paramedics will be here soon. They'll get you stitched up."

Kasey and Bishop helped Collins out of the bathroom and into the living room.

"Shouldn't we check the rest of the apartment first?" Kasey asked.

"No need, Kasey," Bishop replied. "If he was here, we'd know about it. He'd have already taken a shot at us. Besides Tac. Support will be here any moment. They'll sweep the entire building, just to be safe. Let's get Collins to the paramedics and make sure he's stable first."

Kasey nodded and together they helped Collins out of the apartment and into the elevator. At the bottom, they helped him out the lobby and down the front steps of the apartment building.

The street was packed now. One S.W.A.T van had arrived, its officers disembarking and preparing to enter the building. A cordon of police vehicles blocked the street and, in the distance,, the lights and sirens of an ambulance made its way down the street toward them.

One of the S.W.A.T troopers strode over to Bishop. "What have we got, detective?"

"One shooter, heavily armed, likely machine pistols. Shot up an apartment on the second floor. We have two officers down along with a civilian. Shooter hasn't been seen in some time. It's possible he's already escaped but we need to be sure."

"We'll sweep the building. We've secured the perimeter. If he's still inside, he's not getting out."

"Take him alive if you can, Sergeant. We've a lot of questions we need answered."

The Sergeant nodded. "We'll do our best, detective. Armed like that though there is no guarantee. If he fires on us, he'll be neutralized immediately. We'll not be burying any more of our men today."

The ambulance made its way through the police cordon and Kasey waved it down.

As the paramedics disembarked, Kasey briefed them, "This is Agent Collins of the FBI. He's taken a round to the right external oblique. We have an exit wound, so it looks like the bullet has passed straight through. He's lost a lot of blood though."

The paramedic bent down and examined the wound before nodding. "We'll take him from here. Don't worry, Agent Collins. We'll have you stitched up in no time, then it's off to the hospital for further testing."

Two of the paramedics unloaded a gurney from the van and Agent Collins was helped onto it.

The lead paramedic, a rotund man in his thirties, looked at Bishop. "We heard there was an officer down. Is he still inside?"

Bishop's face was downcast as she replied, "We have two men down inside, along with another victim. But they're already dead. There is nothing you can do for them. Get this man to the hospital now."

"It's true," Kasey added. "The three of them have been shot to ribbons. They have no pulse and haven't had one for the ten or so minutes we've been here. There is nothing more that we can do for them."

"But you can ensure this Federal Agent doesn't join them," Bishop replied. "So please, get him to the hospital now."

"Aw, Bishop, I didn't know you cared," Collins replied.

Bishop smiled, a rare thing. Kasey didn't need to be prescient to know what was coming next.

"Don't flatter yourself, Collins. I can't have my inter-agency liaison dying on me... far too much paperwork."

Collins laughed, then grunted in pain. The head paramedic looked at the wounded agent again before replying, "If you insist. We're out of here. Load him up, folks."

The paramedics slid the gurney into the back of the ambulance and in moments it was snaking its way through the police cordon.

Kasey turned to Bishop and smiled.

"What on Earth are you smiling about?" Bishop asked.

"Well, I was joking about Mr. husky voice at the station but I'm not now. I've never seen you so worked up..."

"Kasey..." Bishop began.

"Oh, come on, Bishop. Tall, blond, and handsome there, he's totally into you. If he weren't in that suit, he'd look like a lifeguard from summer break."

"Kasey, don't you dare..." Bishop headed for the squad car.

"Don't what?" Kasey teased as she followed her partner. "You were thinking it. I don't blame you either. I'd let him give me some mouth to mouth any day."

Bishop spun around, the color rising in her cheeks. "Kasey, if you don't cut it out, I'll shoot you myself."

"If you do, just make sure you pop me in the same ward as Agent Collins.

Bishop threw up her hands in submission as Kasey's phone rang.

"Saved by the bell," Kasey chimed as she answered the call.

"Kasey, it's Vida. You need to see this."

CHAPTER 17

Kasey burst into the morgue.

"What have you got for us, Vida?" Looking around, she stopped dead. There was paperwork on every surface of the usually pristine room. Vida had purloined a white board from somewhere else in the station and was hastily scrawling notes across it. "What on earth happened here?"

Vida looked up from the white board. "Oh, Kasey, sorry, I didn't see you come in." He looked around the room. "Yeah, my apologies for the mess. I've been analyzing the dossiers on the killer's targets. I needed a little more room to delve into each of them."

Kasey made her way over to the board. "Found something interesting?"

Vida nodded. "A great deal actually. At first, I thought we were dealing with a killer who is working on a physical profile, hence why all of our victims look so similar.

"In cases such as these, it is easy to draw the conclusion that the killer is trying to right some sort of sleight in his past. Maybe he was rejected by a woman. After killing her, he finds that he is still angry, so he continues to kill women who resemble the one that first wronged him, at least in his mind anyway. At least, that is how these cases present initially.

"But two things have always bothered me with that hypothesis. First, the cold clinical nature of the killings.

Murders that are crimes of passion are messy, the first is certainly. Each of the crime scenes we've seen have been clean, not a shred of discernible evidence left to give us a clue of the killer's identity.

"The second is the changing nature of the murder weapons. In the first, our killer used his bare hands and immense strength to kill the victim. In the second he used a car. Why? It makes no sense. Using a car adds evidence we could trace. Indeed, it led us to his lair at Hudson Road. There he had disemboweled the owner like a wild bear.

"If it weren't for the similar appearance of the first two victims, we wouldn't have even known what we were dealing with. Did I hear correctly that there was an attack on one of the other targets today?"

"Yes. Kelly Sachs. Kelly and her police escort were gunned down in her apartment. They were picking up some medication for her, but the killer was waiting. Gunned down the three of them in her living room," Kasey answered, depressed that another body had been added to the growing tally.

"Gunned down you say?" Vida asked.

"Yes, some sort of machine pistol at close range. The three of them were dead when we arrived. Yet another weapon, a little less messy than his previous victims," Kasey concluded.

"But effective nonetheless," Vida responded as he flipped through the folders on the table. "Kellie Sachs, you said?"

Kasey nodded, but Vida still had his head buried in the folder. "Yeah it was Kellie."

"Aha," Vida shouted, clutching a piece of paper. "She suffered from diabetes. The killer knew sooner or later she'd need her meds. That's why he went after her next. With us scooping up the other victims, it was the most predictable target. All he had to do was wait."

"Any idea of who he might go after next, Vida? If this guy isn't afraid of killing police, none of these girls are safe. Even in custody. We need to grab this guy the next time he sticks his neck out."

"I'll keep looking, Kasey. In the meantime, you should know... I think he's on some sort of deadline..." Vida smiled as soon as the words had left his mouth. "Sorry, no pun intended."

"What do you mean a deadline?" Kasey asked.

"Well, normally you would expect a serial killer to go to ground as soon as they attract any attention from the police. They know that with increased scrutiny they are sure to be caught eventually.

"So normally they go quiet until the heat dies down. That or they move to a new city and start again. This guy, in spite of all the attention, is only becoming bolder. Now he is killing police to get through to his victims. It's a level of determination beyond what you would expect to find. It's dangerous, for us and the killer.

"The fact that he is accelerating his plans in the face of growing danger means he has some sort of timeline he needs to meet. On top of that, the fact that he has stayed in New York City means these targets are not random. He's not just killing young twenty-something brunettes that look alike. He's killing these ones in particular."

Kasey nodded along with Vida's analysis. It made sense.

With Arthur Ainsley's warning ringing in her ears, she asked, "We need a why, Vida. Why is he killing these women?"

She was desperate for any clue that might help her save the girls—and herself.

Kasey feared the reason might be beyond Vida's understanding. Knowing the Werewolf was a magical creature opened a new realm of possibilities, ones Vida would not be familiar with.

Neither am I.

For the millionth time this week, she regretted just how little she knew about the world of magic.

To her surprise, Vida had an answer. "Well, it took me most of the night and all of this morning to figure it out, but I believe I've found the common denominator in all of these targets."

Kasey took heart. "What did you find?"

Vida's cocky smile returned. "As I read through each of the target dossiers I kept running into the same piece of shared history."

"What was it?" Kasey asked, excited that they were getting somewhere at last.

"Not a single one of these girls is a New York City native," Vida replied. "Each and every one of them migrated here from somewhere else in the USA. Not a single one was born here. Do you know what the chance of that is? The chance that of twenty randomly selected New York City residents that not one of them would be a native?"

"One in a million?" Kasey volunteered, taking a stab in the dark. She preferred medicine to math.

"More like one in billions, Kasey," Vida answered, tapping the folders. "This is no coincidence. This is the link. The killer is looking for someone in particular. He may not know who they are, but he knows roughly what they might look like and he knows they have moved to New York and are in their late twenties. I think he is hunting someone in particular."

The revelation was a relief to Kasey. She'd been scooped into the pool of targets because she'd moved to New York after leaving the Academy. There was nothing in her past that would justify sending a killer after her. He must be looking for one of the other girls.

"Great work, Vida. Now we just have to find out which one he is looking for and what it is they know. Perhaps they witnessed a crime, and someone is cleaning up after themselves."

"They're certainly casting a wide net, Kasey, and they aren't shy about it. Killing twenty women just to make sure you got the one you're looking for... it's excessive," Vida replied.

Kasey nodded along to Vida's analysis. "Well, if we can solve this case, perhaps we will solve another as well. Clearly one of these girls is sitting on something useful. Now we just need to squeeze it out of them."

"Yeah that's the same thing Collins said," Vida replied. "Speaking of, where is our towering inter-agency liaison?"

"In the hospital. He was trying to interview Kelly when they were attacked. Took a bullet in the guts for his trouble."

"Oh, that's awful," Vida replied. "Poor guy has only been here for a day. Bit of a rough start."

"Yeah, Bishop is up briefing the chief right now. Doesn't look good when one of the FBI get shot on our watch. Bishop didn't relish the thought of having to tell the chief."

"Yeah...the chief. I wouldn't want to trade places with her now, that's for sure," Vida said, shaking his head. "You don't mess with West. Everyone knows that."

Kasey nodded. With Bishop on the fourth floor and her injunction not to leave the station, Kasey was stuck.

Pulling up a chair, she lifted one of the manila folders off the table. "Mind if I take a look?"

"Not in the least. Maybe you'll spot something I missed," Vida replied, returning to his white board.

Kasey picked up the file and then placed it back down. Rummaging through the pile, she located the one she was looking for: Elizabeth Morrison's dossier.

For some reason, he chose Beth first. If what Vida says about a deadline is true, something about Beth must have stuck out as the most prominent target.

She began digging through the folder. Much of it she was already familiar with. Beth's work history and relationship status, she was all too familiar with.

She continued reading and found a post-it note Vida had left in the file. 'Moved to NYC' was hastily scrawled across it. She scanned through the dossier. To her surprise, Beth Morrison had moved to New York in her teens. She had lived with her aunt until she had finished school. According to the file, most of her family lived in Los Angeles.

Kasey compared herself to the young woman to see if she could add anything further. The pair of them had moved to New York at roughly the same age, and both of them shared the same first name, or at least they had until Kasey had changed hers from Beth to Kasey. Reaching the end of the file, Kasey flipped it shut. That was about as far as the similarities went.

She grabbed the second file. It belonged to Brandy Cahill. Contrary to Beth Morrison, Kasey had almost nothing at all in common with Brandy besides physical appearance. From work history to food preferences, Kasey couldn't find another single similarity.

Eventually, Kasey made her way to the end of the file where she spotted another one of Vida's notes. 'Born and raised in South Dakota. Moved to New York City.'

South Dakota. Now that's interesting. She hadn't known that before. South Dakota and its famous Mount Rushmore were home to the Academy of Magic; it was one of the Arcane Council's best kept secrets.

Kasey had lived there herself as a student in her teens. Was Brandy also a witch? While not an observation she could share with Vida, it may have accounted for why the killer had elected to run her down with a car rather than get too close.

She rifled through the folder and found Kelly Sachs' profile. She had moved to New York City from Florida and had only been living in the city for three years. Reaching her job history, Kasey found something: Kelly had worked as an instructor in a local Kung-Fu Dojo. The recently deceased young woman shared Kasey's passion for martial arts.

That's weird. As she made her way through each of the victims, she found that each one had more in common with herself than they did with any of the other women. Yes, they were all similar in appearance and they had all moved to New York City, but each of them also shared something else with

Kasey that they didn't share with each other. Beth Morrison had the same first name. Brandy Cahill had lived in South Dakota and was possibly a witch. Kelly Sachs loved martial arts.

The realization hit her like a freight train.

The killer was looking for her. He just didn't know it yet.

CHAPTER 18

K asey was dumbfounded. She tried to come up with another explanation, but she couldn't. Maybe it was her prescience, maybe it was just the nagging feeling in her gut, but she knew the killer was searching for her.

Danilo Lelac, one of the World of Magic's most notorious assassins, was hunting her. The Werewolf turned killer for hire had come to New York to find her.

Clearly, he was operating on old information; the presence of such a diverse group of targets explained as much. Unfortunately, that smoke screen wouldn't hold up for long.

If I hadn't caught him by surprise, he'd probably have killed me at Hudson Road. Who would want to kill me?

She wracked her brain for an explanation. It had to have something to do with her magic. Otherwise, why would a creature of magic be hunting her?

Could a normal have hired Danilo?

She thought it unlikely. Whoever it was clearly hadn't seen her in years. The information Danilo was using was over a decade old. If the assassin had known who he was hunting from the beginning, there would likely have only been one body...hers.

The macabre thought raised another.

If I'm to die, will my gift show me that it's coming? Will my gift manifest itself when it matters most?

Glimpses of the future were rare, and her gift was far from flawless, it could not be summoned at will. There was no way of knowing if the absence of a vision meant she was safe or if her gift even functioned like that at all.

In the magical community, prescience was such a rare gift that precious little had been written on the subject. Kasey had tried researching it when she had been at the Academy but most of what had been written was speculation or superstition by those who had no experience with visions whatsoever.

Most magical beings who possessed prescience kept it to themselves. Kasey could understand why. Even at the Academy, her innocent sharing of her visions with others had resulted in intense backlash. Most of her fellow students had shunned her to avoid any unwelcome intrusions into their personal lives.

Maybe they are after me for my gift. Did I see something I shouldn't have?

Her phone ringing interrupted her thoughts. It was Bishop.

She answered it. "Hey Bishop, what's up?"

"Kasey, I'm still with the chief. Can you join us?" Bishops voice was quiet but insistent.

"Sure," Kasey replied. Three visits to the chief's office in a week. This can't be good.

"See you soon."

Kasey got up and made for the door.

"Where are ya heading?" Vida asked.

"That was Bishop. Apparently, the chief wants to see me."

"Again..." Vida said, focusing his gaze on her. "You might consider moving your office to the 4th floor. It will save you some time on your commute."

Kasey laughed as she made her way out of the morgue. She reached the elevator and began pacing while she waited for it to arrive. She ran over the details of the case in her mind over and over. She knew she was close to cracking the case. She could feel it.

The elevator dinged as its doors opened. She stepped inside and mashed the button for the now familiar fourth floor. The trip up seemed shorter than normal.

Stepping out of the elevator, she smiled at Kathleen who was at her desk.

"Head on in, Kasey," Kathleen said, popping a stick of gum into her mouth. "They are expecting you."

"Thanks, Kathleen."

She entered the open office, and then shut the door behind her. Bishop was sitting in the chair nearest to her.

Kasey made her way to the second chair and sat down. She studied the chief. He looked exhausted, a world different to the morning visit with Arthur Ainsley. Now he was deflated.

The Chief stretched his arms before folding them over his chest. "Kasey, thank you for joining us. Bishop has been filling me in on this morning's events."

"I see, chief. How can I be of assistance?"

The chief leaned forward in his chair. "First, I want to hear your take on the situation."

"My take, chief?"

"Yes, your take, Kasey. You are the only one who has even seen this man. He may as well be a ghost. Our technicians have been running through video footage from traffic and store cameras all week. Not even a glimpse of him. I imagine when we are done analyzing the footage from today's shooting, we will still be in the same position. This killer has a knack for coming and going unobserved, but whether we see him or not, the bodies are piling up. Now two of our own have been added to the deceased. I want to know what you think we should do next?"

Kasey sat pondering the chief's question. She'd been wrestling with the same issue all day. Danilo was a ghost. A dangerous one at that. If he could gun down two police why not four? The precinct couldn't protect these girls forever. Slowly but surely, Danilo would make his way through his list, and anyone that got in his way.

"Chief, I fear that this is only the beginning. His increasingly bold attacks show a complete disregard for our presence. Add to that his skill in ensuring no evidence is left behind. We have little idea where he might be now and if we wait for him to strike again, we risk more deaths."

"If we don't know where he is, there is little choice but to wait," Bishop interjected shaking both her hands. "We need to increase the size of our guard details and rotate them in irregular patterns so that we don't give him an opportunity to strike. Eventually, he'll slip up and when he does, we'll be there to take him down."

"That is one option," Kasey said, "but I'm tired of sitting around waiting to find out when it will be my turn."

"What are you suggesting?" Chief West asked, as he leaned forward on one arm.

"I'm suggesting we go on the offensive. Lay a trap and wait for him to take the bait."

"Kasey, we can't go using these potential victims as bait. It's too dangerous. If anything happened, it would be my head," he replied.

"Oh, I'm not suggesting we use one of them, chief. I'm suggesting we use me."

Bishop's eyes widened. "Kasey, are you crazy? We haven't gone to all this effort to keep you safe, just so you can throw yourself back in front of a train."

"Well, it wouldn't be a train, Bishop," Kasey said, turning toward her. "It would be a serial killer. They're very different." As the words left her mouth, she realized just how sarcastic her words sounded. "What I mean is, this killer is flesh and blood. We can stop him. We just need to be a step ahead of him instead of a step behind. With me as bait, we can finally get that chance."

"I'm not a fan, Kasey. If anything goes wrong, you're dead. There's no second chances if this goes poorly," Bishop said, shaking her head.

"If we don't do it, he just waits around for us to get complacent. When that happens, I am still dead and there is every chance others will be killed in the crossfire, just like today."

Bishop went silent and Kasey knew she'd made her point.

Looking at the chief, she asked, "What do you think, chief?"

The chief was quiet. His stare drifted from Kasey to Bishop and back to Kasey. "It's safe to say, Miss Chase, that I'm not a fan of any plan that would put the lives of any of my people in jeopardy. I would much prefer we take a different path, but as that path is yet to present itself, I am inclined to consider your proposal."

Bishop opened her mouth to protest. "But..."

West cut her off. "No buts, detective. I'm about to leave this office and drive across town to visit two families whose husbands and fathers aren't coming home tonight. That's not a visit I ever like to make. It breaks my heart. If we can do anything to prevent such a tragedy from happening again, we must do it.

"I'm authorizing you to proceed. Do so with caution. I'll make available every resource we have, to support you. Be vigilant. If he's willing to kill police, no one is safe, so avoid crowded places. Get him somewhere quiet and take him down hard. If he resists, put him down for good."

"Yes, chief," Bishop replied nodding but her slack jawed expression was difficult to conceal.

"You're excused. Good luck and Godspeed."

Kasey stood up and made her way to the elevator, Bishop only a step behind her.

As the doors closed, Bishop exploded. "Kasey, how could you propose something like that. It's insane!"

Kasey punched the button for the bullpen. "We don't have any other choice, Bishop. If we wait for this guy, he'll pick us off one-by-one. At least this way, we have a chance to take him on our terms."

Bishop frowned. "You realize if we fail, you'll die right?"

Kasey pat Bishop on the shoulder. "Then let's not fail. If it's any comfort to you, I have every confidence in your abilities."

"We are 0-6 with this one Kasey. I..."

"Bishop, it'll be fine. We just need a plan." Kasey tapped her open palm.

"With the way you were talking in there, I figured you had one," Bishop replied.

"I do," Kasey answered. "At least part of one. I just need your help with the details."

The elevator stopped, and Bishop stepped out, leading the way into the bullpen. The mood was somber. Losing two officers in the line of duty was a sobering occasion. One that would not be soon forgotten or forgiven by the Fighting Ninth.

Kasey followed Bishop to her desk. Bishop stopped so quickly, Kasey bumped into her from behind.

Agent Collins was sitting on the corner of the desk.

"Collins, what are you doing here?" Bishop waved her hands around. "You should be in the hospital!"

"I was," Collins said with a smile. "Then they finished stitching me up, so I released myself. I wasn't going to stay cooped up in that wing while you had all the fun."

"I dunno that we can beat getting shot in the fun department, Collins...unless you count getting killed. If so, Kasey here will have you covered."

Agent Collins clapped his hands together. "So, you have a plan? Excellent!"

"Part of a plan," Kasey admitted. "We're still working on the details. We're planning to bait him into sticking his head out. We're hoping that with all the other targets in lockdown, he'll take a swing at the only one he can find—me."

"It's bold, Kasey, but you understand the stakes, right? You could die." Collins said standing up. "It's not for the faint-hearted."

"Either we take a chance to lure him out, or we wait for him to come for me on his own terms. You were there this morning. How did that go for you?"

"Point taken," Collins responded, holding both hands up in a sign of surrender. "What's the play?"

Kasey snatched a piece of paper from the printer and slid it into the middle of the desk. Borrowing one of Bishop's pens she began to sketch a map of the station and its surrounding streets.

"We wait a few hours, then I head home for the night. I have you guys follow me and when he makes a move, we take him down."

"What makes you think he'll be watching the station?" Bishop asked.

"You've seen the files. This guy is paranoid about his surveillance. With most of his targets holed up in here, he's sure to have eyes on the station," Kasey replied, tapping the station on the map.

"Yeah, but if he's watching the station, he'll see our officers getting into position and know it's a sting," Bishop countered poring over the map. "Unless we slowly send them home over the next few hours and station them along your route home. That way we won't raise his suspicions and we'll still have plenty of support in the field."

"I like it," Collins replied. "Very clever. When are we doing this?"

"We'll start sending our guys out now, ensure everyone is in position ready for Kasey to leave. Kasey can head home around 5:30 like usual."

"Maybe I'll head to the gym," Kasey suggested. "That way he'll feel like my routine is back to normal, or I'm just blowing off some steam."

"Perfect!" Bishop replied. "I'll brief our guys. Kasey, you aren't to leave the station until then. Promise me. No sneaky meals, no running off with your sister. We need you here, where you're safe."

Kasey nodded. "Sure. I'll send Vida out if I need something."

"Speaking of food. I'm going to grab a bite," Collins said, standing from the desk. "Hospital food is the worst."

"Don't give me that—you weren't there long enough to be served a meal!" Bishop replied.

Collins chuckled. "Good thing too. That stuff is worse than a bullet. It could kill someone."

As the day wore on, officers trickled out of the station. To an observer, it would appear they were going about their regular duties or heading home as their shifts concluded.

Slowly but surely, they were taking up positions between the 9th precinct and Kasey's apartment. Her route home had been meticulously planned to ensure maximum visibility as she left the precinct and made her way to the subway. The route would allow the surveillance officers from the Ninth Precinct to detect any tails.

Once Kasey reached the station, she would board the 5:45pm to Ridgewood. If anyone followed her from the station, the train would allow them to narrow the possibilities.

On reaching Ridgewood, she would exit the station and take a shortcut through an alley. The alley would present a perfect opportunity for the killer. Thanks to her plan, dozens of officers lay in wait, stationed along the route. If the killer showed his face, he would be taking his meals through a straw for the rest of his life. The Ninth Precinct would not be gentle. If somehow Kasey was caught alone, she had the Spear of Odin and was ready to use it.

Arthur Ainsley wanted Danilo Lelac dead and his true nature concealed. That would be difficult with the majority of the Ninth watching her, but Kasey was sure she could make the body disappear from the morgue before it was thoroughly examined. That would have to do.

She looked at her watch. 5:29pm. Time to go.

She picked up her bag.

"You ready to for this, Kasey?" Bishop asked, appearing seemingly from nowhere.

Kasey startled but tried to hide it. "Sure am... Let's do it."

Collins entered the station's lobby and made his way over to Kasey, before handing her an earpiece and a small broach.

"We'll be with you every step of the way. You'll be able to hear us with this. And we'll hear you through this wireless mic that will transmit via your phone. If you need help, just call and we'll be there."

Kasey pulled out her phone and synced the mic to it, before putting it on. Sweeping back her hair, she fitted the ear bud in her ear.

Bishop lifted her phone. "Testing one, two, three."

Her voice burst through the earpiece.

"I hear you loud and clear," Kasey answered. "So, Fighting Ninth... are we ready to nail this piece of trash?"

The response in her earpiece was deafening.

"Affirmative."

"Hell yeah."

"Got your back, Chase."

"Roger that."

"We'll make him pay."

Kasey took a deep breath as she pushed open the station's double doors. "Alright, let's catch a killer."

If we don't get ourselves killed first.

CHAPTER 19

K asey hit the sidewalk at a brisk pace, not out of fear but out of planning. There was a chance that someone following a similar route to Kasey might raise a false alarm. By weaving through the crowded street, she forced anyone pursuing her to match her pace, thinning the possibilities.

As she made her way toward the subway, she fought the temptation to look behind her. She couldn't risk showing the killer they'd been made. She'd need to trust the Ninth Precinct to have her back.

"Easy, Kasey," Bishop's voice in her ear warned. "We need to give him a chance to spot you."

"Very true," Kasey whispered, trying to ensure her mouth didn't move too much. Talking to herself would surely be a giveaway.

She slowed her pace to a swift stride.

It was 5:30 and the streets were packed with commuters. With this many people thronging the street, she hoped the killer would not act before they sprung their trap.

Danilo was a difficult threat to juggle. On the one hand, he'd shown a willingness to gun down anyone to get to his victim, but to do so on a crowded city street would leave witnesses to his identity. Collins had been too busy staying alive to get much of a look at the masked killer. Likewise, he could hardly shapeshift into his were-form without causing mass hysteria.

Kasey simply hoped Danilo favored preserving his identity over killing a single target.

Bishop's voice whispered in her ear. "Don't look now, Kasey, but we think we have someone on your tail. He's certainly tall. About six feet and wearing a black hoodie. Haven't got a good look at his face yet, but he is Caucasian."

"Certainly looks like our shooter from this morning," Collins chimed in. "Guy does a good job of masking his identity. A ski mask this morning, a hoodie now. This fella doesn't want to be seen, but his size is a giveaway."

"What do you think, Kasey?" Bishop asked.

"I had the same problem at Hudson Road. Got the drop on me too. Size sounds about right but no clue on the ethnicity," Kasey lied.

If it was Danilo, he'd be European, so the suspect certainly sounded promising. She picked up the pace.

"He's matching your speed, Kasey. Not getting too close but not going away either."

"Alright, I'm almost at the station. Let's see what he does." Kasey hit the stairs two at a time. Reaching the turnstiles, she swiped her MetroCard and made her way onto the platform.

"He's taking the stairs, Kasey. We're about to lose sight of him. Morales, have you got eyes on him?" Bishop called.

Morales was pushing a janitor cart around the subway station in a bid to remain undetected. "Sure do. He's just exited the stairwell. He's swiping his card now. He's hot on your heels, Kasey. He'll be on the platform any second now."

"The train isn't here yet." Kasey whispered. "I'm going to make my way down the platform to buy some time."

"Good thinking, Kasey," Bishop replied. "Collins and I are heading to ambush alley. We'll see you there."

Kasey snuck a glimpse over her shoulder in time to spot her tail as he entered the station. The hoodie hid most of his face in shadows, but Bishop wasn't wrong—he was massive. He wouldn't have been out of place in a college football defensive lineup.

He was carrying a bag slung over one shoulder and a newspaper in his hand. She still had no idea what Danilo's face looked like, but her tail was certainly big enough for her to believe he might be the were-beast from Hudson Road.

Kasey wove her way through the press of people on the station's platform.

"Hey!" A jostled businessman shouted after her.

Kasey paid him no heed. She looked down at her watch. One minute. Kasey sensed her tail closing in. Where she'd had to wiggle and weave through the crowd, the man moved like Moses through the Red Sea as commuters parted to avoid being trampled.

Morales whispered over the comms, "He's still closing, Kasey. Hasn't taken his eyes off you since he hit the platform. I'm moving to assist."

Morales abandoned his cart and made his way onto the platform, seeking to intercept the killer.

A whoosh echoed through the subway tunnel as the train pulled into the station. Kasey had run out of platform and the train was still pulling in. No, no, no.

She glanced behind her. Her stalker was still moving toward her. Her pulse raced and she could feel her heart thumping in her chest with every beat.

Closer and closer he came, with Morales hot on his heels. There was a screech of brakes as the train came to a complete halt. Kasey tapped her foot impatiently. With her hand inside her jacket pocket, she rubbed the shard of Odin's spear for reassurance. She imagined for a moment what it would be like to summon the spear's power in the middle of a crowded subway station. Doubtless it would shock her stalker. Likely Morales too.

While the spear gave her comfort, she would need to wield it with care. Arthur Ainsley's vague warning about discovery still rang in her ears. No, the spear wouldn't help here. Instead, she found herself begging for the doors to open.

The doors parted, answering her silent prayer.

She leapt onto the carriage as her stalker came within reach. Weaving between passengers, she made her way up the train. Here in the narrow confines of the subway car, the stalker's size was a disadvantage.

Still he pressed forward. Kasey moved into the second carriage and snuck a glance over her shoulder.

Danilo was only a few steps behind. As he made his way into the next car, he collided with a commuter rising from his seat. Danilo bounced off the commuter and hit the floor.

Kasey raised her eyebrow.

"Son of a..." he called out, rising to his feet, only to come face to face with a man who dwarfed even him.

"Easy, tiger, you ran into me. Why don't you take a seat and stop shoving your way through the car? You can have mine. I'll be getting off soon anyway." The man pointed to the seat he'd just vacated.

All eyes turned to watch the altercation as the two men sized each other up. As the attention mounted, the stalker looked around the carriage weighing his options. When the commuter didn't back down the stalker took the offered seat.

"Appreciate it, thanks," Danilo answered, taking the seat. His tone told a different story, but it was apparent, he had little choice in the matter.

"You're welcome." The commuter waved then disappeared through the crowd.

As he did so, Kasey recognized the familiar face of Officer Henley staring back at her. Henley snuck her a reassuring wink. In his plain clothes, it had taken her a moment to realize just who had come to her aid.

A voice in her ear whispered, "Johnson here, Chase. We have half a dozen officers on this train. If he makes a move, we'll drop him like a sack of potatoes. Rest easy. We've got your back."

Kasey's sigh of relief was audible. Turning away from her tail, she whispered, "Thanks, guys."

"Don't mention it. It's what we do," Johnson replied.

With Henley running interference, Kasey was able to catch her breath. Danilo glanced at her periodically, but he made no further effort to close the gap.

Kasey could have made her way down the train but that wouldn't have served her purpose. She needed Danilo to follow her when she got off. If he lost sight of her, the entire trap might fall apart.

Instead, she stayed in her spot, pulling out her cell to distract herself as she tried to calm down. She would need her wits about her as the most dangerous part of the entire operation still lay ahead. They had found their man, but they still needed to lure him away from the crowd. That way they could take him down without posing any further threat to innocent bystanders.

She flicked through her messages. One from her sister, Sarah, "Hope you're feeling better, Kasey. I'm here if you need me."

Another from her parents read, "Sarah told us you were working with the NYPD. Sounds like a change of pace. Anxious to hear more. Dinner on Sunday?"

Typical Sarah, Kasey thought with a laugh. She'd already spilled to mom.

Kasey had been waiting for things to settle down before she broke the news to her parents.

The subway car slowed as it approached the station.

She whispered into her mic, "Alright, we're here. How are you traveling, Bishop? Tell me you are in position?"

"We sure are, Kasey. Collins and I, along with more than a dozen of New York's finest. Others are forming a perimeter out of sight."

"Good. The train is stopping. I'm bringing him to you now," Kasey whispered.

"Henley, Johnson. Bring your boys at a distance, just in case. If he makes a move on Kasey before she clears the station, put him down."

"Got it, detective," Johnson replied.

Kasey still hadn't spotted the elusive Johnson, but she was sure he was hiding out somewhere on the subway car.

As soon as the doors opened, she was through them. It took all the self-control she could muster not to turn around and check for her tail.

"The target has disembarked." Johnson informed them. "He's still in pursuit, Kasey. Take it away."

"That's a shame," Kasey replied. "I could really use a bathroom right now."

"Kasey!" Bishop's voice cut in. "Don't you dare deviate from the plan. We're here and waiting. Bring him to us."

"I know…I was just saying I could use one, that's all. I'm coming up now, be ready," Kasey replied as she swiped her MetroCard and kept moving. She reached the stairs and started her climb.

Reaching the alley, she didn't even pause. She simply turned right into it and meandered, so she would still be visible when her tail reached the entrance.

The cluttered corridor also ensured Kasey could duck and hide should the need arise. If Danilo tried to go to ground, he'd find that he was cut off and hemmed in.

"We have eyes on you, Kasey. Keep it coming," Bishop called through the earpiece.

Reassured, Kasey pressed on.

"Suspect is at the alley's entrance. He's looking around," another officer announced.

Take the bait, Kasey willed silently. Just a few more steps and the pain and stress of the past few days would be behind her. What was more, the victims and their families would have closure, knowing the animal who'd killed their loved ones had been brought to justice.

"He's in," Johnson's voice called through the earpiece. "He's coming your way."

CHAPTER 20

Kasey turned to face her would-be killer. His sandy hair stuck out from beneath the black hoodie. Kasey could see the recognition on his face as he spotted her in the alley. Even from where she was standing, she could see the corners of his mouth twist into a smile.

Her feet froze as fear overcame her.

Her stalker locked eyes with her and reached for his shoulder-bag.Kasey's earpiece exploded. "He's reaching for his weapon. Take him down."

Her stalker called to her, "Kasey Chase..."

All around them, building doors burst open as the NYPD sprang from their concealment. Bishop and Collins led the charge, guns in hand. Johnson and Henley appeared at the alley's entrance, sealing off any escape.

Surprise was visible on the stalker's face. "What the..."

"Hand's in the air," Bishop called. "You're under arrest. Drop the bag and put your hands in the air."

The stalker looked around at the police closing in around him but didn't move.

Two NYPD officers tackled him to the ground. Rolling him onto his chest, they cuffed his hands behind his back.

The stalker finally found his voice. "What is going on?"

Bishop continued reading him his rights, "You have the right to remain silent. Anything you say or do can be used against you in a court of law."

Kasey made her way over. His shoulder bag lay next to him. Curious to see what it contained, she picked it up and opened it. Inside were a stack of manila folders, but no weapon.

Expecting them to be new targeting dossiers, Kasey pulled out the stack. Her name appeared on a printed label on the top folder.

The stalker looked up from the ground and spotted Kasey with the folders in hand. Wheezing from the weight of the officers pressing him to the pavement, he called out, "Kasey Chase... you've been served."

At that, he gave up and rested his head on the pavement.

Bishop looked at Kasey. "You've got to be kidding me!"

Kasey scowled, holding up the folders. "I don't understand..."

"He's not the killer, Kasey," Bishop said, blowing a strand of hair from her face. "You're being sued. That's why he was following you. He's not our man. He's a Process Server."

"Sued?" Kasey asked. "What on earth for?"

She tore open the folder and read the document.

"That little mongrel. It's John Ainsley. He's suing me for damages relating to his injury." Her voice was a mixture of irritation and disappointment.

All their effort and planning had been for nothing. If anything, the killer had likely watched as they'd showed their hand.

"What do we do now?" Kasey asked.

"We toss this clown in a cell while we make sure his story checks out. It might just be a cover. If it isn't, we're back to square one. Let's get you back to the station so we know you're safe," Bishop replied putting her arm around Kasey.

"And what about this?" Kasey asked, waving the paperwork.

"I can't help you with that. I'm a detective not a lawyer," Bishop said.

Kasey shook her head. A lawsuit on top of everything else. It was just too much. She turned away, worried that she would tear up in front of her colleagues.

An arm wrapped around her shoulders. It was Bishop. "Don't stress. We'll find you a lawyer...and we'll find the killer too. The plan was good. We executed it perfectly. Now we just need a new one."

"You're right. Thanks," Kasey said, fighting to suppress her tears.

"Ride with us back to the station. It'll give you some space to relax and get yourself together. You're doing great. Don't beat yourself up."

Kasey nodded and followed Bishop to the car. The ride back to the Ninth Precinct was a quiet one. Kasey couldn't bring herself to read the lawsuit she was holding in her hands.

She just got irritated every time she thought of it.

So much for Arthur keeping him off my back. Hopefully if we nail Danilo, he'll keep his word. If not, I guess I'll go hunting for a lawyer.

Bishop pulled up to the front of the Ninth Precinct. "Okay, Kasey, I'm going to leave you here, hun. Head inside and get some sleep. We'll work out the details in the morning. I need to get some rest. You should too."

"Yeah, you're right. I've barely slept in days. I could use it," Kasey replied.

"Whatever you do, you're not to leave the station, Kasey. Understood?"

"Yeah, yeah, I know the drill," Kasey muttered.

"Good. Head on inside. I'm going to talk to Agent Collins for a moment," Bishop replied.

Kasey couldn't help herself. "Is that what the kids are calling it these days?"

She grinned as she opened the door.

"Get out of here, you," Bishop said turning a little red.

Kasey leaned down to the window. "Oh, I'm out of here all right. I wouldn't want to interrupt any inter-departmental liaising."

Bishop rolled her eyes and Kasey laughed as she turned for the station.

"Night, Bishop!"

"Night, Kasey," Bishop said, rolling up the window.

It was almost seven and the station was settling into its evening roster. Kasey made her way down to the morgue to avoid having to speak to anyone about the day's failure.

Kasey's stomach growled as she entered the morgue.

"Wow! Didn't realize how hungry I was." Since she was stuck in the station, take out was her only option. Pulling out her cell, she punched #3 on her speed dial.

"Hello, Stromboli's Pizza, this is Giuseppe. How can I help you?" His sonorous voice came booming down the phone line.

"Giuseppe, it's Kasey Chase. I was wondering if I could get a pizza?"

"Ah, Kasey, of course you can. Am I right in supposing you would like your usual, the large pepperoni pizza?"

"Sure would, Giuseppe. I think that will hit the spot nicely."

"Very well. Are you coming to get it, or shall I have it delivered?"

"Delivered, please. I'm stuck at work. So, if you could have it sent down to the Ninth Precinct, that would be magic."

"I certainly can, Kasey. It's the middle of dinner so we are being swarmed, but rest assured our driver will have it to you in a half an hour."

"Thanks, Giuseppe. You're a lifesaver."

"Anytime, Kasey. Enjoy your evening."

The cell line went dead, and she placed her phone on the counter.

Seeing the stack of folders on the counter, she picked them up with both hands and threw them across the room. She'd taken her best shot at nailing Danilo and it had all come to naught. Not to mention, she was being sued by John Ainsley.

Reaching into her pocket, she clutched the Shard of Odin so hard it almost split her skin. How she wished she were face to face with John now. The lawsuit would have to wait, though. In the scheme of things, it was still the lesser of her afflictions.

Danilo Lelac was out there, lurking in the shadows. Sooner or later, he would come for her. Spear of Odin or not, she still had no idea who he was in human-form. One wrong step and she'd end up like the victims lying in the drawers of the morgue. The constant vigilance was taxing her physically, emotionally, and mentally.

This has to end.

She paced the floor. There was no way they could bait Danilo into another trap. There was every chance he'd watched and laughed at their failed sting attempt. No, we need to go on the offensive.

Determined she must have missed something, she went over to the drawers and pulled them open: Beth, Brandy, and Kelly. As she studied the bodies, she ran through each of the murder scenes in her mind once more. She had been over Beth's several times and was confident nothing had escaped her attention there.

Likewise, the hit and run where Brandy had died had failed to yield any insights. Her vision had led her to Hudson Road which had been a blessing. It had almost cost her life but at least she knew what she was up against now. It was a shame Brandy hadn't gotten a glimpse of Danilo; the car's headlights had obscured any hope of learning his identity. So close, but yet, so far.

Kasey walked over to the third drawer. Kelly Sachs. Bishop had been too eager to get Collins to safety, so Kasey had been robbed of the opportunity to examine the scene. Kasey badly wanted to pick apart that apartment. If Danilo had been lying in wait for a while, it was possibly he had left some clue behind.

For a moment, she contemplated sneaking out to revisit the scene of the shootings.

Bishop will kill me. I best wait until morning.

She had never considered herself afraid of the dark but knowing there was a Werewolf lurking in the shadows was certainly weighing on her nerves.

As she stared down at Kelly's body, Kasey realized that in her haste she had not examined her. In fact, she'd never laid a hand on her.

A vision, Kasey thought. Perhaps Kelly had seen something Collins had missed. Right now, anything will help. Anything at all.

Timidly Kasey reached out and touched Kelly's arm.

Nothing happened.

Kasey recoiled as if stung.

What? Of all the times my gift has been a curse, now it chooses to be silent? Kasey was in disbelief. She reached out again and grabbed Kelly's arm. Still nothing.

Kasey stormed away from the drawers in frustration.

"Give me something!" Kasey demanded out loud to no one in particular.

Eying the steel drawers, a thought dawned on her. There was one more body she hadn't considered.

She almost barfed at the thought of the decomposing form in the 4th drawer, Lincoln Stride. The poor occupant of Hudson Road had been dead for days when she had stumbled upon him.

There had been no need for an examination. Lincoln had clearly been murdered. The cause of death was clear too. He'd almost been torn in half by a Werewolf.

Kasey wasn't sure what to expect from the poor man, but she hoped against hope her gift had something to offer.

She crept to the drawer. Taking a deep breath, she held it in as she drew out Lincoln's body.

Lincoln Strode lay there and it wasn't pretty. The refrigerated drawers had helped somewhat but Lincoln had been decomposing when they had brought him in.

Desperate for a clue, Kasey reached out and clasped the dead man's hand.

To her relief, the familiar mist clouded over her vision and the morgue disappeared. When it cleared, she found herself standing inside a house.

She scanned her surroundings. It took only a moment to register that she was standing back inside 65 Hudson Road. The house was cleaner than she remembered, gone were the flies and half eaten food.

She eagerly searched for a clue as to when the vision was taking place. It was before her visit. It was before Lincoln had died; Kasey could see him tidying the house.

The doorbell rang.

Kasey followed Lincoln to the door. From her viewpoint, she could see a large silhouette through the frosted glass pane beside the door.

Don't open it, Kasey thought before realizing the futility of such wishful thinking.

Oblivious, Lincoln opened the front door.

Kasey's mouth fell open in amazement.

There standing in the doorway of 65 Hudson Road... was Agent Collins.

Mist descended over her vision and in a heartbeat, it was gone.

"What?" Kasey exclaimed as the morgue came into view.

A thousand thoughts crashed through her tired mind.

Before she could sift through them, a heavy hand rested on her shoulder.

Chapter 21

A familiar voice pierced her heart. "Kasey."

Spinning around, Kasey came face-to-face with Agent Collins.

"You!" she shouted, struggling to get words out. Collin's presence at Hudson Road could only mean one thing.

"Me, what?" Collins replied, a confused look crossing his face. "Sorry, Kasey, I didn't mean to frighten you. You were just standing there, staring into the drawer."

She tried to back away, but with the cold steel of the morgue drawers behind her, there was nowhere to go.

"What are you doing here, Collins?" she demanded, trying to buy time while she came up with a plan.

"I just came to check on you. You looked pretty shaken up after the sting went bust. I just wanted to see if you are alright," he said, raising a hand to calm her.

"I'm fine." She pushed past him, putting some distance between them.

Her mind raced a million miles an hour.

If Collins had been at Hudson Road, he must be the killer, Kasey thought. My vision could be misleading me again, like it did with Brad.

As she stared at the hulking FBI agent in front of her, conflicting feelings stirred in her chest. If Collins was Lelac, why hadn't he killed her already? He'd had the chance. If he wasn't, she couldn't risk using the Spear of Odin. If she were wrong, she couldn't kill a Federal Agent just to conceal the World of Magic. Kasey was stuck, and she didn't like it.

Collins was at Hudson Road. He knows something. I need to test his DNA. The hair sample we found on Beth's body had something that outed its owner as magical. If it didn't, the ADI would have had no need to mention it. If Collin's DNA had the same non-human markers, I'll know he's a Werewolf. Now I just need him a little more cooperative.

Kasey eyed the stainless-steel tray on the table in front of her. If he's not Danilo, I'm going to have some explaining to do. Whether it was the stress or the exhaustion, Kasey wasn't sure, but she snatched the tray, scattering implements across the table. Swinging it with two hands, she spun toward Collins.

Collins wasn't nearly as surprised as Kasey was hoping. He raised a hand to block the incoming tray. "Kasey, what the hell is going on?"

Kasey drew back the tray and swung again. "You were there. I saw you."

The flat of the tray hit him in the chest, driving the wind from his lungs.

"Where?" Collins answered grappling for the tray as he fought to regain his breath. "What are you talking about Kasey?

Of course I was there. I was with Bishop," he replied, fending off the tray as Kasey made for another swing.

She swung the tray at him again and again. Then she let it clatter to the floor as she delivered a roundhouse kick to his chest.

He hadn't been prepared for that. Stumbling back he caught his foot on the loose tray, sending it sliding across the floor as he narrowly avoided landing flat on his ass.

Before he could recover, Kasey was in his face, launching punches. Unfortunately, Collins was built like a brick wall. The jabs barely made a mark. As Kasey's right hand sailed toward his jaw, Collins stepped back. He was deceptively nimble for someone so large. Her fist caught nothing but air. Collins reached out and grabbed it.

He yanked on her arm, drawing her in. He wrapped his arms around her, pinning her hands to her sides to prevent further attacks.

Kasey struggled to break the grip, but he held firm.

"Now, Kasey," Collins started, as he tried to catch his breath. "Care to tell me what is going on?"

Kasey struggled against his hold. "I saw you there. You were at Hudson Road."

"Hudson Road?" Collins replied.

"Don't play dumb. I saw you there. Number 65 Hudson Road. Lincoln Strode's house. It was days before we even met you," Kasey fumed, raising her foot.

"Oh," Collins replied.

Kasey slammed her foot down onto his. He jerked backwards.

Without mercy, Kasey drove her elbow back into his stomach...right next to his bullet wound from the morning's shootout.

Collins let out a howl of pain. Kasey doubled down, sweeping his legs out from under him and sending him crashing to the floor. She scanned the ground for the tray, then swooped and picked it up. Lifting it high, she went for the knockout— only to find herself staring down the barrel of Agent Collins Glock.

The black steel of the pistol's barrel stopped her dead.

"Okay, Kasey," Collins said, huffing, "if you try to hit me again, I swear I'm going to shoot you."

She dropped the tray, then lifted her hands in surrender.

Agent Collins got up off the floor, eying her warily. "Now if you wouldn't mind explaining what on Earth is going on, I'd really appreciate it."

"I saw you at Hudson Road. You visited Lincoln Strode before he died," Kasey explained slowly. "Tell me how an FBI agent knew who was going to die, days before we even found the body? Explain that one to me, Collins."

Collins jaw dropped. "Ah, you're prescient?" He nodded. "The chancellor didn't tell me that. Could have saved me a beating if he'd mentioned it. I suppose you saw some sort of vision then?"

Kasey blinked. "Wait, what? Chancellor? You know about visions?"

She wasn't sure which question she wanted an answer to more.

Collins looked at Kasey and then the gun in his hand. "If you are done trying to kill me, let me explain. I don't work for the FBI. I work for the ADI. Arthur Ainsley sent me here to look out for you."

Kasey shook with rage. "Look out for me? More like spy on me."

Collins holstered his weapon. "It's not like that, Kasey. The Chancellor may seem callous, but he wasn't going to pit you against a killer on your own and just hope for the best. He sent me for backup."

Arthur's interference caused her blood to boil. Knowing Collins was his lackey did little to raise her opinion of him. "You still haven't explained why you were at Hudson Road. Lincoln Strode is dead. As far as I can tell, you were one of the last people to see him alive."

"That doesn't mean I killed him, Kasey. Do you have any idea who Lincoln Strode was when he was alive? He was the Alpha leader of New York's Werewolf pack. I was there to warn him about Danilo Lelac. I'm not sure how familiar you are with Werewolves, Miss Chase, but they are highly territorial. When the Arcane Council received word of his arrival here in New York, I was sent to warn Lincoln..."

"I'm sensing a but," Kasey interjected.

Collins took a step back and rested his hand on his hip. "Not so much a but, more of an and. The council was hoping for Lincoln's help in tracking Danilo. Danilo may not be from his pack but his presence in Lincoln's territory would not go unnoticed. Danilo is a fugitive, and we were hoping to bring him to justice."

"And?" Kasey prompted.

"And what? He thanked me for the warning but declined to help the Council. Werewolves may be members of the magical community, but after centuries of bad blood, there is still a lot of skepticism between Werewolves and other magical beings. There was no way he was turning over one of his kind, not to us. So, the visit went pretty much as we expected. We left with nothing, which was a shame."

"A shame? What do you mean?"

"Strode was our best chance to catch Danilo. Now he's dead and his pack has scattered. Danilo likely targeted him for that very reason. Now he can move freely through the city. The pack is far too preoccupied to be bothered with a stray. Strode was a stabilizing influence between Werewolves and wizards. Now we'll have to wait and see who succeeds him as pack leader. His death will have far reaching consequences."

"I'm sorry to hear that," Kasey said. "I had no idea."

"There's nothing we can do about Strode now," Collins replied as he squatted down and began to tidy up the trashed morgue. "We just need to take down Danilo before he can hurt anyone else."

"Is there anything else you know that could help?" Kasey asked, joining him in the cleaning. "Your boss wasn't particularly helpful in that regard."

Collins shook his head. "I'm afraid not. While the Golden Wolf is the terror of Europe, no one has seen him in human form and lived to tell the tale. That sting today was the best shot we had at taking him down. I was really rooting for it to work."

"So, if no one has seen his face, he could be anyone...even you?" Kasey asked, testing Collins.

"Sure, why not?" Collins replied, holding up Vida's scalpel that had been dropped in the scuffle. "But if I were out to kill you, you would already be dead."

Kasey couldn't help but see his point. The two of them were alone and it was late. As an ADI agent and a Wizard, Collins could have killed her and been gone before anyone was the wiser.

Besides, he's already taken a bullet to try and save Kelly.

She was exhausted and her nerves were so frayed she'd just beat a wounded agent with a tray. That realization bothered her more than anything else. Her stomach let out a low growl.

"I have some food coming. Want to split a pizza?" she asked.

"I appreciate the offer, Kasey, but I've gotta get some rest. Besides, Bishop and I had a snack in the cafeteria earlier."

"Oh, did you now?" Kasey asked with a laugh. "Smooth moves, Collins. She's going to be mad when she realizes you're not with the FBI though."

"Let's keep that to ourselves for now. Might raise a few questions we can't answer. If you want to grab your pizza, I can clean up for you down here."

Kasey's stomach rumbled again. "That would be great, Collins. I'm going to stuff my face and relax. I'll catch you in the morning."

"Good night, Kasey... Make sure you get some rest," he added.

"Will do," Kasey answered as she dashed out the door. She headed straight for the elevator. the hallway was dark except for the pale green exit lights.

As Kasey pondered on the poorly lit corridor as eerily familiar footsteps followed her down the hallway.

Her mind raced. The darkness, the haunting footsteps.

It was déjà vu.

The shadow wizard.

Kasey spun around, catching only the faintest glimpse of motion before it thumped into her skull.

Her world went black in an instant.

CHAPTER 22

The first sensation Kasey became aware of was the pulsing headache at the back of her skull.

Opening her weary eyes, she saw steel. Rows of steel. It took a moment for her to process what lay before her.

She was in a cell.

Sitting up, she almost slammed her head into the steel above her head. The bars were everywhere.

Not a cell—a cage. What the hell?

The last thing she could remember was leaving the morgue to pick up her pizza. Something had happened in the hallway.

She'd been attacked. The wizard was back, and this time she'd been caught flat-footed.

She felt the back of her head. A sizable lump was forming from whatever had struck her. She blinked to focus her vision, and then took in her surroundings.

She shook her head in disbelief. She was in her apartment. Or more precisely, she was locked in a cage bolted to the floor of the living room of her apartment.

And she wasn't alone.

Just out of reach was a second cage. The unconscious form of Agent Collins lay within. The cage looked almost comical with the large agent stuffed inside it.

Kasey rattled the bars of her cage. Locked.

"Collins," she whispered.

He stirred but didn't budge.

"Collins, wake up," she begged.

He let out a groan as he rolled onto his back. Reaching out, he grabbed the steel of the cage. "What on Earth is going on, Kasey?"

"I don't know. Someone jumped me at the station," she whispered. "They knocked me out, and I woke up here."

Collins nodded. "I heard something in the hallway and went to check on you. Whoever got you, clobbered me too. Feels like my head is on fire."

"At least we are alive," she said. "Now we just have to get out of here."

Collins sat up. "Any idea where here is?"

"That I can help with," she said. "We're in my apartment."

"That's weird. Why would they bring us here?" Collins asked. "When the police realize you are missing, this is the first place they will look."

"Yeah, but that might take hours," Kasey said as she tested the lock. "If it's Danilo, we'll be dead by then."

"If?" Collins asked, his whispered voice rising sharply. "Who else could it be? I was working on the assumption you only had one party trying to kill you."

Kasey sighed. "Well, true, or at least I thought it was, but I had a run in with a wizard in an alley the other night. The jerk tried to kill me and when I broke his nose, he just melted into the shadows and disappeared."

Collins' mouth sagged open. "A wizard, you say? Melted into the shadows?"

"Yes," Kasey replied, "I figured I'd scared him off but now he's back and he's not happy. What I don't get is why we're here and why we are still alive?"

"What do you mean?" Collins asked.

"Well, Danilo has it in for me, that wizard had it in for me. That much I know. I'm just trying to work out why he has kept you alive. Dragging you out of the station must have been a pain, so why go to all that effort when he could have just killed you and been done with it? No offense."

"None taken," Collins said. "It's a good question. I've been working on the assumption that Danilo wants you dead. Have you considered that maybe he wants something else from you and simply killed the others because they couldn't provide it?"

Kasey thought back to her own analysis of the case. Did her gift have something to do with why she was being hunted? Nothing else in her past made sense. Perhaps she had seen something or someone, and somehow that knowledge posed a threat to the Hungarian assassin. It made sense, but for the life of her she couldn't work out what that vision might have been.

"I've thought about it," Kasey said. "I figured it had something to do with my visions. Nothing else adds up. I separated myself from the world of magic years ago. The only thing tying me to it now are the visions. I can't get rid of them. Trust me, I've tried."

"Makes sense," Collins said. "Not great news for me though."

"Why do you say that?"

"Because if it's true, I'm expendable and I'm here for one of two reasons." He leaned back against the cage.

"Like what?"

"One, information. You've probably seen police interrogate a suspect. They often use a method known as the prisoner's dilemma where they separate two suspects and try to get them to turn on each other in exchange for reduced sentences.

"It works like a charm, has for decades. It's no good here though because only one of us has the information he wants. It's possible that he is watching us and hoping we spill whatever it is he is seeking.

"The second option is leverage. When interrogating a suspect, torture is a highly ineffective means of gaining the information you are seeking. Often the target will say anything just to get the pain to stop. Torturing someone else though, that tends to be more effective. Most people can't tolerate watching someone else suffer knowing they could end it. It seems I will have that unfortunate pleasure."

"You paint a grim picture," Kasey said. "How do we know which it is? I don't want to give him anything, but I don't think I'll hold up well to watching you get tortured either."

"It's impossible to tell. He's not here so we have time. The longer we stall, the greater our chance that Bishop or someone else will find us."

"We could always blast our way out of the cages," Kasey said, frowning. "Take our chances in a fair fight. I presume you are a wizard?"

"Of course I am, but we have no way of knowing what countermeasures or hexes he may have in place. We could make it worse for ourselves. We need to get ahead of them, not play into his hands."

"What do you suggest?" she asked.

"Let's work out why he wants you, Kasey. If he's wanting information, talking will buy us time. If he makes a move on us, we blow the cages and take our chances. Deal?"

"Sure." She shifted to make herself a little more comfortable.

As she did so, she reached into her pocket and felt the cold but reassuring silver of the Shard of Odin.

I'm not moving till he shows his face. This ends tonight.

Whichever foe showed their face, wizard or beast, they were going to receive a lesson in Norse history they would remember for the remainder of their very brief life.

"So, Kasey, obviously you've given it some thought. What have you seen in your visions and who have you told?"

"Why does it matter who I've told?" Kasey asked.

"Because it helps us narrow down our choices. If we know what you've seen and who you've told, surely we can trace exactly why he's after you."

"Makes sense," Kasey admitted. She took a deep breath. "When I was at the Academy, I had loads of visions. Something about the concentration of magical beings there made them more frequent, I had visions every day. Sometimes they were about my classmates. One of them was afraid of the dark. Another had an abusive father. Once I had a vision of two seniors fooling around."

Collins nodded. "Go on."

"To start with, I thought being prescient was normal. I figured everyone with magic had visions, so I told my friends about them. At first, they thought it was funny, so I shared more of them. As soon as they realized how far reaching my gifts were, they became afraid.

"People knew that by coming in contact with me, they were giving me a window into their life that they couldn't close or control. So, they shunned me. People didn't want to be around me or even talk to me for fear I would learn something they didn't want to share.

"After that, I started keeping things to myself. Unless I thought it was dangerous, like someone's life was at risk. Then I shared those with my teacher or the headmaster, just in case."

"Anyone else?" Collins prompted.

"I saw a guidance counselor at school for a few months. Mrs. Dalsorth. I shared a lot of the visions with her so she could help me deal with them. But once I left the Academy, I left the world of magic behind and I stopped talking about them. I changed my name, I moved to New York. I don't want anything to do with that world. I didn't choose to be prescient. If I have a vision, I say nothing. I don't want to destroy any other lives."

"Hmm, being prescient is a marvelous gift, Kasey. Most magical beings would trade places with you in an instant," Collins replied.

"Feels more like a curse," Kasey said. "Nothing good has ever come of it."

"That's not true. If you are using your gift at work, I'm sure those insights will save lives. Think of the girls who are in protective custody now. Without you, they might all be dead. Your gift saves lives and will continue to. If you use it wisely."

The thought cheered Kasey up as much as her current circumstances would allow. "Saving lives is great, but it was my gift that put them in danger in the first place."

Collins shook his head. "That's only because someone must have shared something. If you've not shared anything since you left the Academy, something in one of those visions from the Academy must be what they are after. They must be what they want to keep hidden."

"That's easy to say but hard to break down. It's like trying to pick a needle in a haystack."

Collins took a labored breath. "Not every piece of hay is worth killing for though. Who likes who, and other embarrassing student gossip won't result in an assassin hunting you down more than a decade later. You saw something, something worth killing for."

Kasey wracked her brain. "I got a fellow student busted for selling drugs. One of the seniors overdosed and almost died. When I visited her in the infirmary, I saw a vision. The student who sold them, Frank Halsetto, was expelled."

Collins shook his head. "Bigger, Kasey. We're looking for something bigger."

"Kristyl, one of my friends. Well, her mom was having an affair with a teacher. When I told Kristyl, everything fell apart. The school found out and Mr. Janston was sacked. Unfortunately, he ran away with Kristyl's mom and once more I got the blame for everything."

"That won't be it," Collins said, shaking his head. "Did you ever see anything bigger? Maybe a politician or celebrity caught in some sort of scandal? Did you ever see anyone killed at the Academy and know who the culprit was? Did you ever have a vision about a business with shady practices? Have you ever seen a vision of the future? Money, murder, sex, or speculation. These are the sorts of things people kill for, Kasey. Did you ever see one of those and tell someone about it?"

Kasey perked up. "I did see the future once... At least, I think I did."

Collins' forehead wrinkled. "What do you mean think? You don't know? What did you see?"

"I have had the same vision many times. I think it's the future. I'm standing on a street when I hear an explosion. All around me people start panicking. The explosions continue as a thick oily green mist descends across the city. Buildings crumble and collapse under the strain. People everywhere are injured or dead. It was horrifying.

"I kept seeing it, so I did some digging. Nothing like it has ever happened. Not in modern times, anyway, and the city was definitely modern. I thought perhaps it was a vision of something that hadn't happened yet. More than a decade later, it still hasn't.

"Sounds stupid, I know. Even for the prescient, seeing the future is rare. Seeing something more than a decade in the future is unheard of. My teachers told me it was just a nightmare, something that would go away in time."

"And did it?" Collins asked.

"No," Kasey answered firmly. "I saw it again on Monday."

"That must be it," Collins said. "You saw it, the attack on New York City. That must be what they are after. What else did you see?"

A chill ran down Kasey's spine.

"I didn't say New York, Collins," Kasey answered, staring at him. "I've never said New York... Not to anyone..."

CHAPTER 23

K asey stared at Agent Collins, but his face was impassive.
The attack still lay in the future. There was only one way Collins could know that the attack was to take place in New York City. He had to be a part of the organization plotting it.

Since seeing her vision Kasey had kept detail of the location to herself. She had not mentioned it to her teachers or anyone else at the Academy. Not even Sarah knew.

Most importantly of all, Kasey knew she was right. The sickening knot twisting in her stomach told her she was right.

In a moment of crystal clarity, Kasey understood what was happening.

The spate of murders across New York City were not random or capricious. Nor were they the acts of some violent sociopath or serial killer. They were cleverly planned and meticulously executed to remove the one person who knew what was coming.

Me.

Word of her vision had continued to spread. No longer was it simply an anecdote about a crazy young girl at the Academy. Someone had heard the story of the horrendous attack and recognized it for what it was—a threat to their carefully laid plans.

To protect their interests, they had done the best they could to track her down. Using all the knowledge and information they could glean from the Academy, they had sent Danilo after her to silence her once and for all.

Unfortunately for the other innocent victims, their passing resemblance to Kasey had put them in harm's way. Whoever was behind the attack was willing to go to great lengths to assure its success. They were willing to kill anyone who fit their profile. Whether they were prescient or not seemed to matter little.

In that moment, Kasey knew she was dealing with someone far more ruthless than a serial killer. Whoever was responsible for Danilo, they were the true threat. Not just to herself, but to all of New York City—and possibly the world.

Kasey looked at Collins. In her heart, she knew who she was dealing with. "Danilo Lelac I presume."

Collin's mouth twisted up into a sinister smile. "What gave me away?"

"You knew too much, and you overplayed your hand," Kasey replied. "There is no way anyone could have told you that the vision was of New York unless they were a part of it."

"I could have guessed," Danilo replied, "After all, you live here in New York. It makes sense when you think about it."

"Only to a sociopath," Kasey replied. "Most people flee from danger, not run toward it. After all, I fled the Academy, didn't I?"

Danilo reached forward and pushed open the door of his cage. It was unlocked. Getting to his feet, he stretched. The cage had been too small for his massive frame.

Approaching Kasey's cage, he loomed over her. "A crazy person or a hero. Is that what you see yourself as Kasey? A hero?"

Her hand clenched around the shard in her pocket. She willed Danilo to step closer to the cage. "No, not a hero. I'm just a woman who wanted to be left alone. I left your world and made a new life. I can't help the visions. I didn't even know the attack took place in New York until this week. So, call it fate or destiny or serendipity, I don't care, but you... you made a horrible mistake."

Danilo Lelac smiled. "What was that?"

Kasey's voice was quiet but firm. "I left your world, but you dragged me back in. Now you will have to live with the consequences. Rest assured, you won't have to wait long, and when I'm done with you, whoever sent you is next."

"Done with me. Kasey?" Danilo's voice echoed his disbelief "You're insane. Do you have any idea how many people I've killed in my career? I am the Golden Wolf and you're an Academy drop out. You'll not be done with me, but I'll be done with you. Now tell me what I want to know, or others around you will start to pay the price of your poor judgment. Starting with your parents."

To demonstrate his point, Danilo walked over to the table and picked something up. It took Kasey a moment to register what it was–her cell phone. Danilo began punching out a text.

"Hey, just having a bit of a hard time lately. Any chance you and Dad could swing by my place? I could really use a chat." Danilo spoke in a mocking imitation of Kasey's voice.

Kasey shook the bars of her cage. The last thing she wanted was for her parents to be brought into harm's way.

Her phone vibrated.

"Oh, would you look at that," Danilo said with a grin. "They're on their way. 'I'll be there in half an hour.' How sweet. The ball is in your court, Kasey. What they find when they get here is up to you. My employer wants to know exactly what you saw in your vision. Tell me, or I swear I'll still be here when they arrive and tomorrow the police will have three bodies instead of one. Your choice."

Kasey seethed with frustration as she beheld the man who not only had killed four people but now threatened the life of her family and her own. Kasey tried to hide her hands that were shaking visibly.

"Oh, fancy that?" Danilo remarked. "I guess you feel some fear after all. Bishop thought you were unshakable. Glad to know you are human too. Don't worry, fear is a natural reaction to your current circumstances."

What Danilo didn't know was that the trembling wasn't fear. It was rage coursing like fire in her veins. She had only felt this mad once before and she had put John Ainsley in the hospital as a result.

There will be no hospital for you, Danilo.

Kasey calmed her mind and focused her thoughts on a singular idea: the cage surrounding her. "Ffrwydro."

At her command, a wave of arcane energy exploded out of her like an angry storm.

There was the tortured shriek of steel on steel as the cage twisted and contorted before snapping altogether. The metal bars showered the apartment in a storm of shrapnel. Danilo dove over the nearby sofa to take shelter.

She rose to her feet, the arcane energy slithering back into her.

No sooner had the apartment gone still than Danilo was on his feet, with his gun in hand, pointed directly at her.

Kasey stared down the pistol's barrel, but this time, she was ready. Not caring how the Arcane Council felt about her actions, she let loose. "Dwrnyrawyr!"

The concussive force struck him in the chest and threw him into the wall. His gun skittered across the floor of the apartment.

She scrambled for the weapon. Danilo shoved away from the wall and charged after her.

With a triumphant cry, Kasey dove for the gun. She grabbed it and pointed it up at him.

She pulled the trigger.

Click.

In desperation, she pulled the trigger three more times.

Click. Click. Click.

Danilo laughed. "It's not even loaded, Kasey. I don't need a gun to kill you."

Before she could react, he dove on top of her.

She tried to roll free, but Danilo was too quick. They tumbled across the apartment floor, fighting each other for the upper hand.

Kasey gasped as Danilo grabbed her by the throat. She let out a savage kick, driving her foot into the gunshot wound in his side.

I bet he's regretting doing that now, Kasey thought. Danilo must have wounded himself to dispel any suspicion after the Kellie Sachs shooting.

He groaned in pain and Kasey used the opportunity to roll free. As she did so, she crossed paths with one of the steel bars of her cage. Grabbing the piece of steel, she sprung to her feet.

Danilo rose to his feet, but Kasey was waiting. With all her strength, she swung the steel bar at Danilo.

The bar struck home with a satisfying crack. Danilo was knocked backward onto the floor.

To Kasey's horror, Danilo simply shook off the blow.

"You really have no idea what you are dealing with, do you?" He turned onto his stomach and rose to his feet. "My people have lived in the harshest climates this world has to offer. We have fought tooth and claw for centuries just to survive. You don't stand a chance, Kasey. You never did."

His arms began to swell, as did his chest. Danilo, or Collins as Kasey had known him, had always been large but Kasey watched in silent amazement as he grew before her eyes. His shirt tore apart as it failed to contain his burgeoning physique.

The pallor of his skin darkened to a golden brown as his jaw distended. In seconds, the transformation was complete. Kasey found herself face to face with the beast she'd met at Hudson Road.

While she had known what Danilo was, watching the transformation had mesmerized her.

"Oh..."

Kasey's sentence was cut short as Danilo let out a bellowing roar that shook the apartment.

He leaped forward.

Kasey sidestepped but Danilo was quicker, delivering a punishing backhand. Kasey tumbled across the room.

It was times like this that made Kasey wish she had stayed in the Academy. Battle Magic and Dueling weren't really subjects the Academy labored over with its younger students. Had Kasey finished her senior years, she would have taken both. Now she would just have to improvise.

"Pêl Tân," she shouted as she stretched out her hand toward Danilo.

A swirling sphere of fire coalesced above her hand before soaring across the living room toward him. Danilo sidestepped the arcane assault, but it still struck him in the shoulder.

He howled as the flames seared his skin and set his golden mane alight. Ignoring the wound, he charged at her. He struck again, his deadly claw arcing toward her stomach. Kasey had seen the aftereffects of such a blow. It was the attack that had killed Lincoln Strode. She half-jumped, half-tumbled over the lethal claw.

The razor-sharp talon caught her in the thigh. It sliced straight through her favorite jeans and into her leg.

She gritted her teeth against the pain and collapsed to the floor as her injured leg refused to take her weight.

Danilo seized the moment and pounced. He swung at her again. She rolled out of the way, but he trapped her to the floor. He snapped his teeth scant inches from her face.

She grabbed Danilo by his throat as she strove to keep the snapping jaws at bay. It was a losing battle though. He drew back his paw for another strike. There was nowhere to go.

Kasey panicked and uttered the first spell she could think of.

"Dwrnyrawyr!"

Danilo was too close to dodge the blast and it caught him dead in the chest.

His claw found nothing but air as the blast threw him straight up. Kasey smiled in satisfaction as Danilo struck the roof, splintering the plaster. Then he began to fall, right back at her.

"Oh, gravity, you bitch." She reached for her pocket as Danilo plunged toward her.

He readied his claws as he plummeted at her.

Kasey watched as the mass of teeth and claws descended. She ripped the Shard of Odin out of her pocket and pointed it at Danilo.

"Afpvi at Odin!"

The spear rang, its ancient magic activated once more. The shard shot out into a wicked point, and the elegant inscription carved by Odin himself rose to the surface.

The Golden Wolf began to flail, but it was too late. Ignoring the pain in her leg, Kasey raised the spear toward the falling Werewolf. With grim focus, she drove the spear home. Danilo howled as the spear plunged straight into his chest, impaled by his own weight.

The bulk of the falling Werewolf knocked the air from her lungs. She rolled on to her side and dumped Danilo onto the floor.

He groaned but didn't move.

She yanked the Spear of Odin free and struggled to her feet.

Danilo lay on his side. Worried that it was a ruse, Kasey used the spear to roll the Werewolf onto his back.

A low growl escaped his mouth. As he looked up at her looming over him with the spear, he raised a claw to try and fend her away.

It was a feeble attempt. The Spear of Odin had done its work well and Danilo was fading fast.

"Is that fear, Danilo?" Kasey asked. "It should be. You might be the Golden Wolf, but to the spear of Odin, you are simply another mutt falling before Odin's wrath."

As Danilo's strength failed, his frame shook and then began to shrink. Before her eyes the Golden Wolf faded, leaving only

Danilo lying there in his human form. Blood seeped from the wound in his chest.

"Who sent you, Danilo? Who wants me dead?"

Danilo shook his head. "I'll never talk."

"If you aren't talking, I have no reason to keep you alive," Kasey threatened.

"There... are worse things than death, Kasey Chase. You... have... nothing... on me."

"What does it matter? You're about to die. Why protect them? They sent you to your death."

Danilo took a labored breath "You asked if I was afraid, Kasey. I am. Just not of you and certainly not of death. There are far worse fates, as you'll soon discover. I wonder if you'll see yours coming."

"Very well, you'll certainly see yours." Kasey replied, raising the spear. "What about the wizard that tried to kill me? Is he with you?"

Danilo let out a wet gurgling laugh. "No. I don't play well with others. Seems the Master shopped this little job around. Good luck with him."

Kasey shook with indignation. "Master, what master?"

Danilo's lip curled as he ignored the question. "When you meet the Master, you'll need more than an old spear. He's going to flay you alive."

After everything that had happened, she was taking no chances. Drawing back, she drove the Spear of Odin straight through his heart.

Danilo went limp against the blade, his eyes closed forever.

Kasey drew out the spear and held it aloft. Danilo's blood vanished, somehow absorbed into the blade itself.

Before she could ponder the ancient weapon's strange behavior, a piercing wail filled the night.

Sirens.

CHAPTER 24

Kasey glanced around her apartment. It looked like a bomb had gone off. The furniture was in disarray and shards of Kasey's cage were scattered everywhere. One piece of steel was embedded in the wall by the front door.

Both the roof and wall still bore the scars of Danilo's impact, and the assassin himself lay dead on the living room floor.

She wasn't sure how the police had tracked her down so quickly, but she was glad they had. It was reassuring to know Bishop had her back.

It was in Kasey's best interest however, that no one take too close a look at the body. Particularly Vida. He would surely run tests and the spear wounds would be difficult to explain away, not to mention any traces of DNA resulting from Danilo's Werewolf heritage.

She looked around and weighed her options.

I need to clean this up and fast.

The sirens drew nearer. They would be here any minute. Subtle magic had never been her strong suit, so Kasey opted for a spell with which she was becoming increasingly familiar.

"Pêl Tân."

Flames soared from Kasey's outstretched hands and struck Danilo. She didn't stop there. Turning on the rest of the apartment, she channeled her frustration of the past week and ensured there would be no evidence left to collect.

Soaring spheres of flames struck the sofa, the walls, and the carpets which caught fire. Kasey ran for the door. From the safety of the doorway Kasey watched as her small world went up in flames. Fortunately, she'd never owned much and the little she had would be easily covered by insurance.

As the flames grew, Kasey knew the threat her fire posed to the rest of the building. At this late hour there would be families and children asleep.

Kasey grabbed the fire extinguisher from behind the door. She could extinguish the flames with magic but that wouldn't leave the right trail of evidence for the police to find.

Pulling the pin, she squeezed the trigger. Foam and mist burst from the hose, drenching the flames. She made her way around the small apartment, targeting the base of the flames to combat the growing inferno.

She had only made it a few steps into the living room when the small extinguisher ran dry.

"I may have overdone it," she whispered as the flames before her continued to rise. Discarding the empty canister, she focused her mind on the fire before her. "Diddymwch."

There was a hissing noise as the flames dissipated. Thick smoke threatened to suffocate her, so she abandoned her effort and the war-torn apartment.

Slamming the door behind her, she raced down the hall. The red fire alarm caught her attention, and she came to a halt.

She broke the glass and pushed the button. Just for good measure.

The wailing alarm filled the night air. If any of the buildings occupants had managed to sleep through the ruckus, the alarm would surely wake them.

She ran down the three flights of stairs and out the front door to find half a dozen squad cars cordoning off the street.

She spotted Bishop as she was fastening her bullet-proof vest.

Bishop turned toward her, then her eyes widened. She jogged over, still working on the vest. "Oh, Kasey, thank goodness. We thought he had you. Why did you leave the station?"

Kasey threw arms around Bishop as her emotions got the better of her. "He did. He grabbed me at the station and brought me here. How did you find me so fast?"

Bishop patted Kasey on the back. "Well... that might have been me. I was worried you might do something stupid, so I had our tech guys put a tracker in your phone just in case. Good thing I did. It would have taken us hours to find you. Where is he?"

"He's dead," Kasey replied. It felt surreal to hear herself say the words.

She'd never expected to take another person's life, even in self-defense. Now as the adrenaline faded she felt the weight of what she had done.

"What happened?" Bishop asked.

"I was in the morgue when I realized who he was," Kasey began, taking care to leave out a few key details. "We fought but he got the better of me. When I woke up, I was here. He tried to kill me, but I had the homecourt advantage. Darn near burned the place down but I got him."

Bishop looked up at the smoke billowing out of the third-floor window. "Who was he, Kasey?"

Kasey looked down at the pavement, not sure how to break the bad news. "It was Collins. He wasn't FBI, that was just a cover. He staged the shooting this morning to throw us off the trail."

"What?" Bishop's face trembled.

"I'm sorry, Bishop. I wish it wasn't true. But he admitted it in the end. He killed the others and he was going to kill me too. It had to be done. I'm sorry."

Bishop shook her head. "You have nothing to be sorry about, Kasey. I just feel so stupid that I fell for it."

"We all did," Kasey said. "But he's dead now. He'll never hurt anyone ever again."

There was a scuffle at the police cordon.

"Kasey, Kasey," a woman's voice called.

Kasey turned to see her mother running toward her, her father only a step behind.

Jane Stonemoore was the matriarch of the family. In the tradition of Stonemoore women, she was an intimidating figure. Slender but with piercing gray eyes and dark hair that was slowly turning silver with age.

Kasey knew where she got her fiery temperament from, Jane had never lost a step and would happily contend with anyone who argued otherwise. Ralph, her father, was the calm to her mother's storm. Quiet and reserved, he happily yielded control of the family to his wife, as was tradition.

Jane swept through the crowd and drew her daughter into her arms. "Kasey, you had us so worried. We saw the smoke and the sirens and thought the worst. We are so glad you're safe."

Kasey burst into tears, sobbing into her mother's shoulder. The strength and cool facade she had forced herself to wear this past week came crumbling down.

The tears came quick and Kasey just let them out.

Kasey felt a hand on her shoulder. It was Bishop. "Kasey, why don't you head home with your parents? We'll clean up here. Take as much time as you need. We will get your statement when you're good and ready. No need to rush things. I'm sure the chief will understand."

Kasey nodded. "Be careful up there. I think I got most of the flames but there is a chance I missed some. The smoke was pretty thick."

Bishop laughed. "The fire department will be here soon, don't worry. You should go get some dinner. Unfortunately, I think someone else had already taken your pizza when you didn't show up to claim it."

In the commotion, Kasey had forgotten just how hungry she was.

"Thanks, Bishop," Kasey stammered. "Call me if you need anything, even if you just need to talk."

"Will do, Kasey. For the time being, you just get some rest. I'll talk to you soon."

Her parents steered her through the crowd.

Leaning toward her, her mom whispered, "So pizza is still the clear favorite?"

Kasey laughed. It was a strange contrast to the tears that were now drying on her cheeks. "Yeah, mom, always."

Jane pulled her tighter. "Arturo's it is then. We'll get a booth and you can tell us all about it."

They helped her into the car and then drove off, leaving the smoldering apartment behind.

CHAPTER 25

Arturo's was one of New York's hidden secrets. A pizzeria in the heart of Queens, its entrance lay concealed in an alleyway just around the corner from the New York Hall of Science.

Accessible only to those who knew magic, it was a refuge from the hubbub of New York's night life. Kasey and her parents took a seat in their favorite booth. It sat opposite a large glass window that looked into the kitchen. From the booth, the chef could be seen creating his masterpieces.

In a normal pizzeria, a chef might toss his dough. As a child at Arturo's, Kasey had been mesmerized watching the dough levitate before the window as Arturo worked both magic and art into some of the finest pizza New York City had to offer.

Kasey hadn't been to Arturo's in years. It had been a part of the world she had sought to leave behind but sitting here now brought back so many memories.

Arturo smiled when he caught her eye. Scooping a ball of dough off the counter, Arturo flicked it behind his back like a basketball player tossing a pass. The dough sailed up and over his head before coming to a hover above his outstretched hands. Kasey watched in familiar wonder as the dough spun, forming a perfect base. At Arturo's command, ingredients sailed off the counter and onto the base, arranging themselves according to Arturo's most exacting specifications.

The sound of a throat being cleared drew Kasey's attention away from the window.

Johnson and Clarke, the two goons from the ADI, stood beside the booth.

"Miss Chase, we're sorry to interrupt but we've just been by your apartment..."

Kasey couldn't believe it. After everything she'd been through, they just couldn't leave her alone.

"And what, Clarke?" Kasey erupted, cutting him off. "Something about it not to the Council's liking? When you set me up to die, you weren't very specific. I thought torching the place along with everything I owned would be sufficient. What did I miss, Clarke?"

The ADI agent looked nervously at his partner before continuing. "It's nothing like that, Kasey. I assure you; the ADI feels you did admirably. You should be commended for your success."

Kasey's eyes narrowed. "I feel a but coming."

Johnson chimed in. "When you return to work, if you could also ensure any evidence of Danilo's true nature is erased, we would be most appreciative."

Kasey nodded. "Of course. I was already planning to."

"Wonderful," Johnson replied. "Well, once again, we apologize for interrupting your meal. We hope you have a pleasant evening."

The agents turned and made for the door.

"Ahem," her mother said, stopping them in their tracks.

The agents turned.

"Come here, boys," her mother said. Her voice was firm and unequivocal.

If the agents took umbrage with being called boys, they weren't game to show it.

As they approached, her mother stepped out of the booth and made her way over to them, not stopping until she was right in their face. "Do you know who I am?"

"No, ma'am," Clarke responded nervously.

"Ah, that explains a lot. Let me enlighten you. I am Jane Stonemoore of the Caerdydd Stonemoores."

Clarke and Johnson's face fell as they stepped backward.

"Yes, those Stonemoores, and if I ever find out you've put my daughter in harm's way again, you will spend the rest of your lives frozen in amber lying in the bottom of the harbor. ADI be damned, you'll rue the day you crossed my path, do you understand me?"

The agents nodded as they beat a retreat from the restaurant.

Her mother returned to her seat and looked expectantly at Kasey.

Her father broke the silence first.

"Kasey, it seems you've had quite the week. Care to bring us into the loop?" Her father's calm demeanor never wavered.

"Sure, Dad, but before I get into it, I should mention something."

"What is it, dear?"

"Ernesto asked me to put in a good word for him. He said you had a jeweled box he's been trying to trade you for, for some time now."

Her father laughed. "Tread carefully with Ernesto, Kasey. He is as sly as he is shrewd. Were it only a jeweled box, I'd have parted with it years ago. I know as well as he does what is inside."

"Oh, yeah?" Kasey raised her eyebrow. "What is it?"

"It is a subject for another time. Pray tell, what did Ernesto give in exchange for that favor?"

Kasey pulled out the shard out of her pocket and laid it on the counter. "He loaned me this."

Her father leaned forward to examine the silver shard. "What is it?"

"That, Dad, is Gungnir. The Spear of Odin."

Her dad bolted upright. "You're kidding me. It couldn't be."

"I assure you it is," Kasey said. "It saved my life."

Her father nodded slowly as he leaned back in his chair. "Ernesto must be more desperate than I imagined. Start at the beginning, Kasey. Don't leave anything out."

"Well," Kasey began, "you remember when I was at the Academy. You remember my nightmare, the one of the destroyed city?"

"Yes, of course," her mother replied.

"It turns out it wasn't a nightmare. It was a vision and it is the future not the past..."

"Pardon me," Arturo interrupted as he set down his masterpiece.

The aroma of the freshly baked pizza wafted through the pizzeria and Kasey could feel her mouthwatering.

"Arturo, you haven't changed a bit!" Kasey declared.

He smiled. "Oh, if such were true, Kasey. I am an old man now, but you are the same charming young woman you always were. We've missed you."

Kasey felt guilt at having not visited the pizzeria for almost a decade. "I'm sorry, Arturo. I've missed you too. Things have changed, though. You'll be seeing a lot more of me than you are used to."

Arturo bowed. "I hope so. It would be our pleasure."

Her mother beamed as Kasey hoisted a slice of pizza into the air, the melted mozzarella stretching beyond belief as she sunk her teeth into the slice.

"Mmm." Kasey was in heaven.

"You were saying, dear?" Her mother prompted.

Kasey gulped down the mouthful of pizza. "Oh, yeah. Sorry, mom. It all started on Monday with a murder."

The End

War is coming to New York City. Kasey has seen it in her visions, but her second sight has painted a target on her back, and it's attracting attention. The supernatural sort. As she hunts for answers, she finds herself a hostage. Her captors?

Genghis Khan, William Shakespeare, and George Washington. Experience the adventure in **Life Is For The Living (click here or scan the QR code below).**

Looking for the paperback version? Click here or scan the QR code below.

Want some bonus Kasey Swag?

I put together some bonus reading material on the Academy of Magic, the school Kasey went to as a young witch. You can find it at the link below.

Academy   of   Magic   Bonus   Swag   -
https://www.books.samuelcstokes.com/academyofmagic

THANK YOU FOR BEING HERE

I hope you enjoyed Dying to Meet You. It is the first title in my Conjuring a Coroner series. It's one of several set in my Arcanaverse.

As a self-published author, I don't have the huge marketing machine of a traditional publisher behind me. In fact, it's just me (a giant introvert), my laptop and a desire to share my stories with the world.

Since I began this journey though, I have discovered I have something far greater on my side. **You. The incredible readers that share my worlds and my love for a good book.**

Like you, I love to read and know you have a never ending To Be Read List. I just wanted to take a minute to thank you for being here.

Your support means the world to me, and it makes a difference in helping me bring these adventures to life. Every time you tell a friend about my series or share something about it on social media, it helps me reach readers and share more stories like this with the world.

When you leave honest reviews of my books, it also helps other readers take a chance on me. It is the #1 thing you can do to help me (and Kasey) out.

If you have enjoyed this book, I would love it if you could spend a minute or two to leave a review for me (it can be as short or as long as you like, and the link below will take you to the right page).

Review This Book

Thank you, your support makes all the difference!

Until next time!
S. C. Stokes

P.S. I know many readers are hesitant to reach out to an author, fearing that they might get ignored. I am a reader at heart and know how you feel. I respond personally to every Facebook message and every email I receive.
You can find me on:
Facebook
Bookbub
Email: samuel@samuelcstokes.com

You can also visit my website where you can join my newsletter and receive some bonus stories set in this universe that are only available there.

Scroll on for a taste of Conjuring A Coroner 2: Life is for the Living.

LIFE IS FOR THE LIVING

A piercing scream split the room.
  Kasey turned to see a flood of movement at the door as the sound of a submachine gun split the air.

One of the room's ornate chandeliers came crashing to the floor. Glass scattered in every direction.

There was a shrieking stampede as the gala's guests tried to flee from the gunfire.

A dozen assailants, all dressed identically in black from head to toe, streamed into the hall. Their only distinguishing feature were their masks, each bore a caricature of a famous historical figure.

Kasey glanced at the rear entrance she had used. Three more assailants had taken position in front of it.

They each carried the same weapon, Heckler and Koch MP5 submachine guns. She couldn't help but feel bothered at the sensation of being killed by the likes of cartooned Abraham Lincoln and Thomas Jefferson.

The patrons fled before the intruders only to find others blocking their path.

As one, the surging mass of patrons retreated toward the immense ice sculpture that ran along the wall of the exhibit.

A voice rang out through the hall. It carried over the noise like a ringleader at the circus. "Ladies and gentlemen of New York City. Welcome to this evening's main event. We are so glad that you could all join us, and we are even more thrilled that you have turned out in your finest attire."

The voice was coming from the southern end of the hall, the main entrance.

Kasey strove for a better view. One of the masked intruders advanced on the guests. His movements were confident and self-assured. He held his submachine gun at the ready. In spite of his short stature, his powerful voice commanded attention. Over his face he wore a caricature of the Mongol warlord Genghis Khan.

"As you are no doubt beginning to wonder, this is a robbery," he announced. "You may call me the Khan. It is as good a name as any, I suppose."

The Khan raised his gloved hand in a closed fist. Extending one finger, he waggled it before the room. "I must inform you that this evening, while we intend to rob you blind, we have no intention of you being harmed in the process."

Kasey stumbled as one of the gala guests backed into her. Steadying herself, she considered kicking off the silver stilettos but didn't want to draw any undue attention.

The Khan continued pointing to the entryway. "If you follow our instructions, you will all remain as healthy as the moment you walked through those doors." He paused before continuing. "Should you disobey our directions, we will have no choice but to make an example of you.

"We're more than aware that this event is well attended by New York's finest, doubtless accompanied by your personal security. Before any of you are stupid enough to draw your weapons, you should consider the following.

"One, you are outgunned. Whatever concealed weapons you are carrying, they are no match for an MP5.

"Second, know that a number of our party have brought along a little surprise." The Khan opened his jacket as he spoke, revealing a vest covered in pouches and wires.

Kasey's heart went into overdrive, it was beating so fast it threatened to leap out of her chest.

"We're carrying enough C4 to turn everyone in this room into a fine red mist. It will likely also bring down the roof of this historic structure, and none of us want that. So, for the sake of this fine museum, and your lives, I must insist that none of you make any sudden or foolish moves," the Khan continued.

"Our vests are rigged with dead men switches. Should anything happen to us, they will detonate, as will a number of other charges that we have set around the museum.

"We would much rather be considered thieves than murderers, so I must request that you follow our instructions to the letter."

More than a dozen of the armed men stood in the exhibition hall, corralling the gala guests, forcing them away from the safety of the doors and the halls that lay beyond.

There was movement to her right: the pop superstar she had seen emerging from her limousine earlier. Her previous confidence was now gone, and a look of abject terror had replaced it. The star hid huddled behind her private security.

The security guard looked at the Khan advancing. Glancing behind him at the wall, he must have realized they were running out of room. He reached inside his suit coat and drew a pistol.

Before the security guard could raise the weapon, the Khan's submachine gun answered the threat.

The shots hammered into the security guard's chest. He dropped like a rock. The diva screamed and forced her way deeper into the safety of the crowd.

As one, the guests backed away from the fallen guard fearful that in proximity to him they might be next to draw the wrath of the Khan.

The Khan approached the guard who was lying on the floor. He cocked his head.

Kasey looked closer. Wait, there is no blood.

"Oh, you are wearing a vest. That was lucky for you. I promise the next one will bring some sense into that thick skull of yours. Draw a weapon again, and I will kill you."

The Khan picked up the pistol off the ground and tucked it into the back of his pants "I think I'll keep this one just in case. I wouldn't want anyone else getting any foolish ideas."

Addressing the crowd, the Khan continued. "Ladies and gentlemen, I'm going to need you to form a line against the wall. Step behind the tables there.

"Keep your hands where we can see them at all times. If we see any of you using a phone, be it a text a tweet or a phone call, rest assured we'll kill you.

"If the police show up, there will be a shootout and spoiler alert, many of you will also die. So, it is in your best interest to cooperate so that we may leave, and you can resume enjoying the remainder of your evening."

The Khan addressed the cowering patrons. "Now I must insist that we relieve you of any jewelry or other items of value in your possession. In case your perception of value differs from mine, value includes: your wallets, watches, and jewelry. You can keep your expensive threads though. We aren't barbarians.

"Now if you could remove your personal effects and hand them to my companion Shakespeare. He will collect them, and we will be on our way. Does anyone have any questions?"

No one was bold enough to say a word. The man that had been identified as Shakespeare advanced toward the group.

"Get behind the tables and line up!" The Khan demanded.

The gala patrons filed through the tables and began to form a long line running parallel with the wall.

Shakespeare released his grip on his weapon. The MP5 dangled in front of his chest, suspended by a leather strap that ran over his shoulder. With his hands free, he pulled from his backpack a large black sack and made his way to the end of the line.

"You heard the Khan, folks. Wallets, watches, and jewelry. Toss 'em in the bag and no one gets hurt."

Kasey shuffled backward disturbing a patron. Turning, she found herself eye level with a man's chest. Surprised, she looked up into the face of Arthur Ainsley.

Arthur looked past Kasey as he addressed John. "Son, are you alright?"

"As good as can be expected, given the circumstances," John whispered back.

"Well, Miss Chase, fancy seeing you here. To what do I owe the pleasure?" Arthur asked quietly.

"I came to speak about our deal, Arthur," Kasey glanced at John as she spoke, "but it seems that may no longer be necessary."

"Glad to hear it. We have more pressing matters at hand," he answered, turning his attention back toward the assailants.

At the Khan's direction, several gunmen disappeared back into the museum.

Shakespeare continued working his way down the line of patrons.

The guests greeted him with mixed responses. Some trembled as they handed over their wallets, necklaces, or earrings. Others wept as their nerves frayed from the tension in the hall.

Shakespeare came to a stop in front of an older woman in a striking scarlet gown. Her long blonde hair had a tinge of silver running through it. In spite of her current circumstances, the woman was defiant.

Shakespeare pointed at her hand. "The ring too, ma'am."

The woman shook her head. "No. This was given to me by my late husband and I will not part with it. The earrings are worth far more, and you already have those. Take them and be on your way."

Shakespeare leaned forward. "There is no room for negotiation here. ma'am. Put the ring in the bag or you'll be joining your husband in the afterlife."

The woman shook her head. Kasey could see the determination etched into her face. The ring wasn't going anywhere.

Beside the woman, her security guards bristled.

Obviously sensing the rising danger, one of them turned to her. "Mrs. Cardston, we can always get you another ring, but there's no bringing you back."

The woman didn't budge. "No, Stanley, I was married with this ring, and if this young thug wants it, he is going to have to take it off my cold dead body."

Kasey couldn't help but admire the woman's grit. From her position, she could see Stanley's left arm slowly moving behind his back and she knew what was coming.

If Shakespeare made a move, there would be bloodshed.

The Khan watched patiently as the exchange played out before him.

Kasey's keen observational skills had picked up the subtle movements as the other security guards in the room weighed their chance of survival.

Even if they cooperated, there was never any guarantee that they would walk out of the room alive. A promise from armed thieves was hardly something one could stake their life on.

The situation was deteriorating but Kasey was at a loss as to how to stop it. There were far too many bystanders to use her magic unobserved.

Her heart pounded as a trickle of sweat ran down her face. She knew what was coming next. Not because she'd seen it in a vision, but because she could feel it in the room.

The tension in the exhibition theater rested on a knife blade and even the smallest nudge would see it descend into chaos and bloodshed.

Discovery as a witch versus death at the thieves' hands. Should it come to it, Kasey was determined to do her part, knowing her magic might make all the difference in saving lives.

Behind her back, she opened her palm and began to focus her thoughts on the armed thieves before her. As her power gathered she felt a firm hand on her shoulder.

Turning, she found Arthur Ainsley staring down at her.

"Don't you dare," he whispered. "When will you learn Kasey? Your choices will damn us all."

Arthur Ainsley towered over Kasey. His voice was quiet but unyielding. "I mean it, Miss Chase. We have an entire hall full of witnesses here. You will not expose our entire community just to save a few pieces of petty jewelry. It's just not worth it."

"It's not just jewelry, Arthur. There are lives at stake here. Can't you see it? This place is about to blow, and when it does, people are going to die."

She felt time in the room slow to a crawl. She almost expected to see a vision, but nothing came.

Shakespeare shook his outstretched hand at Mrs. Cardston. "Last chance. Give me the ring!"

The woman shook her head.

Shakespeare had had enough, he reached for his MP-5. "I told you already, this is not a negotiation."

Before Shakespeare could raise his weapon, Stanley had his gun in hand.

At point blank range, there was no chance of missing. The pistol bucked twice. It was lights out for Shakespeare as he collapsed in a heap. His bulletproof vest did him little good; Stanley had shot him through his mask.

Patrons ran screaming from the bloodshed as the hall dissolved into madness. As the chaos unfolded, Kasey shrugged off Arthur's warning and summoned her power.

Kasey's troubles are just getting started, don't miss out. Enjoy the epic adventure today!

Also By S.C. Stokes

Conjuring A Coroner Series

A Date With Death

Dying To Meet You

Life Is For The Living

When Death Knocks

One Foot In The Grave

One Last Breath

Until My Dying Day

A Taste Of Death

A Brush With Death

A Dance With Death

Urban Arcanology Series

Half-Blood's Hex

Half-Blood's Bargain

Half-Blood's Debt

Half-Blood's Birthright

A Kingdom Divided Series

A Coronation Of Kings

When The Gods War

A Kingdom In Chaos

Made in the USA
Middletown, DE
29 November 2022

16367410R00130